When the Circus Came to Town

ALSO BY LAURENCE YEP

CHINATOWN MYSTERIES

THE CASE OF THE GOBLIN PEARLS
Chinatown Mystery #1

THE CASE OF THE LION DANCE
Chinatown Mystery #2

THE CASE OF THE FIRECRACKERS
Chinatown Mystery #3

DRAGON OF THE LOST SEA FANTASIES

DRAGON OF THE LOST SEA

DRAGON STEEL

DRAGON CAULDRON

DRAGON WAR

EDITED BY LAURENCE YEP

AMERICAN DRAGONS
Twenty-Five Asian American Voices

When the Circus Came to Town

LAURENCE YEP

DRAWINGS BY SULING WANG

HarperCollinsPublishers

When the Circus Came to Town
Text copyright © 2002 by Laurence Yep
Illustrations copyright © 2002 by Suling Wang

www.harperchildrens.com

Library of Congress Cataloging-in-Publication Data

Yep, Laurence.
   When the circus came to town / Laurence Yep ; drawings by Suling Wang.
      p.   cm.
   Summary: An Asian cook and a Chinese New Year celebration help a ten-year-old girl at a Montana stage coach station to regain her confidence after smallpox scars her face.
   ISBN 0-06-029325-X — ISBN 0-06-029326-8 (lib. bdg.)
   [1. Self-esteem—Fiction. 2. Frontier and pioneer life—Montana—Fiction. 3. Chinese New Year—Fiction. 4. Circus—Fiction. 5. Chinese Americans—Fiction. 6. Smallpox—Fiction. 7. Montana—History—Fiction.] I. Wang, Suling, ill. II. Title.
PZ7.Y44 Wh 2002   2001039290
[Fic]—dc21   CIP
                                                                            AC

Typography by Andrea Simkowski
1   2   3   4   5   6   7   8   9   10
❖
First Edition

In gratitude to the real Pirate Ursula and her bloodthirsty crew—
Moony, Hacker, Roscoe, Bumbus and Tooey—for all their advice.
Sometimes even when I didn't want it.
And to Pirate Cory, the future Scourge of the Seven Seas.
—L.Y.

Contents

PREFACE

I would never have dared try to make up a mulitcultural tale like this. However, truth is often stranger than fiction and, in this case, delightfully so. The story is based on real events that happened in Trembles, Montana.

CHAPTER 1

The Back of Beyond

I live at the Back of Beyond. At least that's what Pa calls it. Folks who don't know any better call it Whistle. That's because when someone rides through town, it's gone between the pucker and the first note of the whistle.

When I was no bigger than a wink, Pa took me piggyback out of Whistle. On his shoulders I felt a mile high.

His legs seemed so long that he crossed a hill in one stride. And his shadow seemed to sweep right out of Montana and straight across a thousand miles to the Pacific Ocean.

Finally he stopped. "Look at those hills in the bad-lands, Sugar. They look just like melted candy. And the river forgets its way and gets lost. There's magic all

1

around us because we live at the Back of Beyond."

"The Back of Beyond," I repeated slowly.

"In the winter the snow only comes up to my waist, but it comes all at once. And look at that sky. There's nothing between us and Heaven."

I wrapped my arms around his forehead and leaned back even more. The sky was so blue that it made me ache inside, and so big and deep that there was no end to it.

You couldn't get me to live anywhere else—not for a thousand dollars. Not for ten thousand. There was always something to keep me hopping. We ran a stage-coach station, so there were horses to tend. I never gave them names though or got too friendly with them. They could be gone with the next stagecoach.

And when a stagecoach came in, didn't we jump! There were a hundred things for a body to do, and all of them had to be done at once. Sometimes I helped Pa change the horses. Sometimes I helped him load and unload packages. A lot of times I helped Ma serve meals to the passengers.

When chores were done, I could walk through a meadow. After a rain was best, because the sage smelled the freshest. Or I'd give an ear to the larks in the meadows along the rivers. Or in the spring I could pick lupines until my arms ached.

And there were always stories to read. My teacher, Miss Hardy, had all these books. By the time I was nine, I'd read every one.

But all my best friend, Susie, could talk about was the Little Ladies of Boston series. Susie was a year older than me. She'd read them and sigh. "I can't wait to visit my grandmother some year. She says I can stay the whole summer in Boston. They got a park with a real carousel. Then I'll get to do everything like the Little Ladies. Not like here. There's nothing to do in Whistle."

Susie's grandmother always sent her the latest dresses and toys. So Susie showed off a little too much sometimes.

I'd read the Little Ladies books too, and all the girls did was wear lots of clothes and drink tea. So I just shrugged. "You can't do anything but be polite and say 'Yes, ma'am' and 'No, ma'am.' And it's please this and please that. And you have to sit up straight all day. It sounds more like jail to me—except in jail you get to scratch when you itch."

"How you talk, Ursula," Susie said. "They don't wear pretty dresses in jail."

"No, because it's too hot in the summer. They dress convicts sensible in just a shirt and pants," I said. "There, I got you!"

"I can't talk to a person who's got no sense," Susie said, and went off in a huff.

I was smarting, though, from the things she had said about our town. So later, when I went for a walk with Pa, I asked him if he would like to live in Boston.

He shook his head. "Not for a million dollars, Sugar.

Everybody locks their doors there. And everyone's a stranger who wouldn't give you the time of day."

"Susie says they got all these museums," I said.

He shook his head even harder. "And they plant those museums and houses so close to one another that they can hardly see the sky. A gopher's got a better view from his tunnel."

"And they got all these fancy restaurants," I said.

"And fancy prices, too. You can pay a month's wages there and come away hungry." He patted his stomach. "Give me your ma's cooking anytime."

I kicked at a rock. "So you like it here?"

"Rugged folk like rugged places," Pa said.

I grabbed one of his suspenders and let it go with a *whack*. "Like you and Ma?"

Pa swept me up in his arms and whirled me round so fast that my head just about spun away. "And like you."

Who needed a carousel when they could have Pa?

CHAPTER 2

Pirate Ursula

The summer I turned ten, Pirate Ursula landed at Whistle.

Passengers were always leaving things behind. Usually it was hats and parasols and books and magazines; but one forgetful person even left a jar with his mother's ashes.

Another fellow left a penny dreadful called *Dead Man's Treasure*. The cover showed a skeleton clutching a chest of gold. If Ma had found it, she would have chucked it in the stove. Any stuff I thought was promising like that she always said was fit only for fuel.

I hid it, though, and read it as soon as I could. It was chock-full of stories about Pirate Dan and his band of cutthroats and their battles with the evil governor of this island.

Later, when I got together with my friends, Susie fanned herself and said how she was going to Boston next year. "Then I'll really have something to do. I can't wait."

My second-best friend, Peter Schultz, was my age. He heaved a real big sigh. "My uncle lives in San Francisco. He says he'll take me out to the ocean."

"Well," Susie announced triumphantly, "my grandmother's going to take me to the circus."

Peter and I just about died of envy. We all wanted to see a circus powerful bad. I used to save the discarded newspapers or magazines that had stories about the circus so the others could read them too. There were real lions and folks flinging themselves through the air on trapezes. The circus was the one thing that might make me leave Whistle.

Peter, though, had to top Susie. "Well, when I get big, I'm going to live in the city. Then I'll see the circus every day."

As much as I wanted to see a circus, that was too much. Imagine leaving Whistle?

"Neither of you has the sense God gave you," I scolded them, and I repeated what Pa had told me.

Susie planted her fists on her hips. "That shows how much you know, Ursula. There's zoos and trolleys and parks and statues. And lots more wonderful stuff to see."

A notion began itching inside my mind about something else Pa had said; but at first I couldn't say what.

"Why, we got plenty of stuff here too."

"Like what?" Susie asked, all saucy like.

I kept scratching and scratching my head as if that could really satisfy the itch inside me. "Like . . . like a lot of things."

Susie tossed back her head. "Show me one."

And then I suddenly remembered what Pa had said long ago about the Back of Beyond. "You want one?" I looked around and then nodded toward a hill. "See that? What's it look like?"

Susie shrugged sullenly. "Like a hill."

"Well, I see a bird with blue and red and yellow feathers," I said. Then I pointed at one that was all silver and gray. "And how about that one?"

"A horse," Peter said. He always picked up a game quickly.

"It's sort of like magic here." I pointed again. "Now take that hill there."

Susie frowned. She was always slow to pick up a game. "I guess a drum."

"And there's a boat," Peter said.

I spread my hands. "See? It's like a giant baby put his toys down. We live in the giant's playroom."

Susie wasn't going to give up, though. "But we can't play with hills. They're too big. So there's still nothing to do here."

"There's plenty," I snapped.

"Like what?" Peter demanded.

7

"Like . . . like . . ." And suddenly I had an idea. "Like pirates," I said. "They go out on their big boat and take treasures." And I hauled out the penny dreadful from my sleeve. After just one chapter, even Susie had to allow Boston couldn't hold a candle to a pirate boat.

"We could be the Scourge of the Seven Seas," I said.

"We don't have one sea, let alone seven," Peter complained.

"You leave that to me," I said.

Then we went back home to my kitchen. Ma was busy baking. I got clean rags and tied them around our heads. Then we got Pa's old army canteen. I put root beer into it.

"Now we need to swipe some provisions for our voyage," I said.

Ma took some cookies out of the stove. "You may have some of these."

"Thank you," Peter said and started to hold out his hand.

I slapped it. "Don't you know any better, Cutthroat Peter? Pirates don't ask. Not the ferocious ones, anyway."

Ma just smiled. She was good about my games. "Please yourself then." She put some cookies on a plate and set it on the windowsill. "I guess I'll just let these cool off."

I put a finger to my lips and nodded for my crew to follow me. We crept outside under the window. Then we stood up slowly. I slipped a gingersnap off the plate.

"Our first plunder," I whispered.

"Cookies aren't treasure," Susie said. She was real slow at this game.

"They are if you're starving, Killer Susie," I said.

"I haven't eaten since breakfast," Peter said. "And that was an hour ago."

Susie grumbled that she guessed she didn't have anything better to do. So she swiped some cookies too.

Then I led my crew into the stable and found an empty barrel. "Help turn it over on its side," I said.

"What for?" Susie asked.

I told myself to be patient. Susie couldn't help it if she didn't have any imagination. "We need a boat to sail away."

Peter's eyes lit up. "I want my own boat."

We wound up rolling three empty barrels out of the stable and away from town.

We went so far that I couldn't see our stagecoach station. All the buildings looked like little wooden boxes drifting on a golden sea.

"How much farther?" Peter puffed.

"Not far," I said. I led them to a gully. Its sides were gentle slopes. I crawled into my barrel. "Now let's get away from the evil viceroy, Deadly Dan."

When I leaned forward, the barrel started to roll. It bounced in the air when it hit a rock. And it kept going faster and faster, right across the floor of the gulch. It went partway up the other side and then rolled back.

I heard a whoop and a rumble. I knew Peter was in his barrel too. When my barrel stopped, I poked my head out. The whole world was spinning around.

Then I heard Susie shout, "Ramming speed." I pulled inside and waited. The rumbling grew louder. Suddenly there was a big bang as her barrel crashed into mine.

We both got knocked out of our barrels. "Try doing that in a city!" I grinned.

"I couldn't." Susie laughed.

The next day Emily and Sam wanted to join. They'd heard Peter talking. When we rammed, I taught them to shout, "No quarter!" Which is pirate talk for no mercy.

On Saturday everyone came into Whistle to shop. Harry came down from the coal mine. His pa managed it. Matilda and Klaus came in from their farm. John rode in with his family from the Circle-T ranch.

By the end of the day, our pirate crew had the whole school of eleven children. They ranged in age from Felicia, who was five, to Andre, who was sixteen.

I borrowed empty barrels from all over town—from the stable, from the store, from the hotel. Then we had to escape from Deadly Dan's prison.

We had a lot of adventures, and I came up with our own secret signs.

At the end of every day, Peter would ask, "What's the heading, Captain?"

And I would tell him, "Chase the sun, Mister Cutthroat."

Then I closed my eyes. I could see us sailing toward that old sun. The sails would catch the yellow light and shine so bright, it would hurt a body's eyes. The ropes would gleam like chains. And our whole ship would turn to gold.

That summer we sailed most everywhere—from the Sandwich Islands to the South Pole and all the places in between.

Susie and Peter stopped talking about leaving.

CHAPTER 3

At the Back of the Back of Beyond

That September, school got off to a roaring start. The first essay was on what we did that summer. Miss Hardy, our teacher, raised her eyebrows when she read about our pirate adventures—even though I took out most of the blood and thunder. "Oh my," she said, "oh my."

But then I got the smallpox. My head started to hurt like someone was hammering inside my skull. Then I started to burn so fierce, blisters broke out all over me.

My parents reckoned I caught it from one of the passengers who passed through our station.

None of my friends could visit me.

They all wrote me a letter, though:

The games aren't the same without you.
Get well soon, Pirate Ursula.
Your Bloodthirsty Crew

I wished I could play games too. I wished I could do anything, but I was so hot and weak, I couldn't stir. I just lay there like an empty feed sack.

Hank, the stagecoach driver, would ask about me. He was the best driver in ten states. He was used to shouting all day over the sound of galloping horses. I could hear him plain as day through my door. "How's my angel Ursula?" he would boom.

Sometimes he left penny candy for me. It was pretty good even when the dirt from his pocket got on the pieces.

After the fever broke, it was about all I could do to walk. But I was right curious. When the scabs broke, I could feel little pits in my skin.

I was real shaky when I stood up, and I walked stiff as a marionette to my bureau. When I picked up my little mirror, I stared at my reflection. There were holes all over both my cheeks. I looked like I had slept on a brush so the bristles had marked my face.

I rubbed at them. They were real deep. They wouldn't go away.

Ma found me rubbing my face.

"They won't go away, Ursula," she said quietly.

"You mean not for a while," I said.

She folded her arms. "I mean forever."

"Why?" I said, beginning to cry. "What did I do?"

"Sometimes these things happen, Ursula," Ma said. She tried to hug me, but I scooted into my bed and hid under the covers.

Pa found me there. "I can tell you now, Sugar. We thought we were going to lose you. You're lucky to be alive."

"I don't feel lucky," I said from under my blanket. "My skin's going to heal good as new."

While I waited, I was still weak. But as I lay there, I told my skin to get pink and smooth again.

Ma started to look real tired, though. She was trying to take care of me and the restaurant at the same time. I felt real bad about being such a bother.

Finally Pa hired a Chinese to cook and serve meals. His name was Ah Sam, and he came to us all the way from San Francisco.

It didn't sit too well with folks in town. I could hear them complaining to Pa. They said Chinese used a drug called opium. They would cheat and steal. They said a lot of other things too. Pa said an old friend had recommended him. Ah Sam was as clean and honest as they came. He would also work cheap, so we could afford to hire him.

Most folks said they wouldn't trust any Chinese. I felt

the same way. So when he came, I didn't go to meet him. I just peeked out my door. I had seen Chinese before, but they were always passing through town. They usually kept to themselves when they ate at our station.

The cook was a small man with long, slender fingers. His skin was a light tan, and his eyes were strange. But his hair was the funniest. It was shaved on the crown so his forehead looked real big. In back, though, he wore his hair in a long pigtail. Ma called it his queue.

He smiled when he saw me. He looked so odd, I closed my door real quick.

I was mad at my parents for bringing a foreigner into our station. He was going to be around all the time. The notion was like a pebble in my shoe. It poked and prodded and made me squirm.

Of course, my parents couldn't help it. They'd hired Ah Sam because of me. So mostly I was mad at me.

The next day Ma brought me the first breakfast Ah Sam cooked. His pancakes were fluffier than Ma's. I didn't tell her, though.

I'd hoped that he'd be a rotten cook. Then my parents could fire him.

Miss Hardy sent my homework around, but that never took me long. When I had read all my books each three times, I got really bored. I missed my friends. I could hear birds passing overhead on their way south. Mostly I missed going outside.

Pa gave me his harmonica and taught me how to

play. "If you can't see your wild birds, maybe you can make music like them."

I wrinkled my nose. "No bird ever sounded like your harmonica."

"But no bird ever sang a tune for dancing," he said.

At first I learned so I could humor him. He taught me a lovely lullaby, "Sweet and Low." The words were by a poet named Tennyson.

When I got a handle on that tune, I learned more, mostly sea chanteys that could arouse my bloodthirsty crew. I'd play them when my skin got pink and new.

Finally the doctor said I was well and could go to school in a week.

I felt my face. "I'm not well yet."

The doctor looked at Ma and then back to me. She must have warned him. "I'm sorry, Ursula. You're as well as you're ever going to be."

"Then you don't know anything, you quack!" And I pulled the covers over my head.

"Ursula, you apologize to the doctor right now," Ma said. "He stayed up nights with us." And she tried to yank the covers away.

But I kept hold of it good and tight. "I'm staying here until my skin gets better."

"Don't worry," the doctor said. "It's just going to take her awhile to get used to the notion."

Ma kept on apologizing, though, as he left.

After that I was bound and determined to heal. The

other smallpox patients listened to the quacks and gave up before they healed completely. But I was Pirate Ursula. I'd make my skin get better.

I'd spend the whole day just wishing and hoping and praying. Then I'd look in the mirror, but the little holes were still there. I didn't let that stop me, though. I just wished and hoped and prayed all the harder.

When Ma or Pa would try to get me to go to school, I'd whip out my harmonica and play as loud as I could. Eventually they'd give up and leave.

But one day I got powerful thirsty. There wasn't any water in the pitcher on my bureau, so I went out of my room. I had to cross the big dining room to get to the kitchen, where the water would be in a crock.

Too late, I saw a stagecoach had come in. Usually the passengers bellow and thump like a herd of buffalo. But this group must have been tired, because they had been real quiet.

A passenger with a thin mustache pointed at me. "What happened to you, little girl? Your face looks like Swiss cheese." And he started to laugh. And then the other passengers did too.

I ran back into my room. But no matter how I covered my ears, I could hear them all laughing.

Pa came in after he had seen the stagecoach off. He smelled of horses.

"I don't want to talk, Pa," I said from under my covers.

"Ma says she heard someone making fun of you,"

Pa said. "There are donkeys in the world like that man, but most people aren't donkeys."

I rolled over on my side away from him. I felt like a monster. "I don't want anyone to see me."

I'd been wrong when I'd told Peter and Susie there was magic in Whistle. How could there be with all the donkey people in the world?

I had to find someplace safe. Someplace where no one could make fun of me ever again. Someplace beyond the Back of Beyond. It would be Pirate Ursula's last voyage.

Of course, I couldn't go to school. Ma and Pa coaxed and argued and scolded, but I stayed put. So Miss Hardy still sent my homework to me, and I did it in my room.

Usually my pirate crew left it with Ma or Pa. But one day, they knocked at my door. I stood behind it and said, "Just leave it."

I waited until I thought they were gone. Then I opened it to get my assignments.

Peter and Susie were still there, though. "We miss you—"

They stopped when they saw my face. Their eyes grew big as doorknobs. You would have thought they had seen a monster. Pa was wrong. Even my friends were afraid.

"Oh, Ursula," Susie said, "what happened?"

I slammed my door shut and ran into bed and hid.

So they went outside and stood by my window. "We're sorry," Susie called.

"Your parents warned us, but it still caught us by surprise," Peter said.

"It's really not so bad," Susie added.

"I saw your faces," I said.

"Pirate Ursula," Susie coaxed, "we just wanted to tell you that your crew misses you."

"Deadly Dan is running wild," Peter added.

They looked like fuzzy shadows through my curtains. I thought they were making secret signs, but I couldn't tell what they were.

Then I realized that if I could see them, they could see me, too. So I hid under the covers. "Go away! Go away!" I yelled.

Pirate Ursula was dead now. There was only Monster Ursula, and Monster Ursula did not go outside. There was only one place she belonged. Someplace where no one else was. Someplace at the Back of the Back of Beyond.

Finally Ma came in and yanked off the covers. "You'll suffocate under there."

"Give me the covers. The curtains are too thin," I complained. I tried to get them back so I could hide again.

Ma sighed. "I know you're upset, but you can't hide all your life."

I didn't know how to tell her about Monster Ursula. And I didn't know how to tell her I had to live at the Back of the Back of Beyond.

"Yes I can," I insisted. "I am going to have to stay in my room for the rest of my life."

Ma argued some, but Monster Ursula could be just as stubborn as the old Pirate Ursula.

So Ma cut up an old blanket and sewed it. Then Pa hung it over the window. My room was dark as a cave now. No one was ever going to make fun of me again.

The weeks went by and Monster Ursula hid. Sometimes, though . . . sometimes I'd listen to the noise outside. And I'd hear the ghost of Pirate Ursula whispering to me to peek out. I'd fight the urge as long as I could.

But finally I'd lift a corner and look at the street. Cowboys clopped by on their horses. Dusty miners came in for gunpowder. The farmers rattled by in their wagons for supplies. Whistle might be small, but it was the only town for a hundred miles. All these things were happening just outside my window; yet as far as Monster Ursula was concerned, they could have been on another planet.

Sometimes I saw my friends run past. I wanted them to remember me as Pirate Ursula, not as Monster Ursula.

So I made sure to close the curtain before they could see me.

When I heard them laugh, though, I wished I could do something about the ache inside.

CHAPTER 4

Ah Sam

Peter and Susie always asked to see me when they dropped off my homework. My old crew just couldn't understand that their captain was gone. There was only Monster Ursula. And she lived someplace where they couldn't go. Someplace past the Back of Beyond.

Monster Ursula stayed there until they left.

After a while my room felt like a jail cell. But that was going to be my world for the rest of my life. When I had read every book a dozen times, I thought I'd get bored to death.

Because I had nothing better to do, I began to play my harmonica a lot. I didn't play any more sea chanteys, though. Those days were done.

Pa liked it when I did "Sweet and Low."

One day he sang along. He had a nice high voice:

"Sweet and low, sweet and low
   Wind of the western sea,
   Low, low, breathe and blow,
   Wind of the western sea!
   Over the rolling waters go,
   Come from the dying moon, and blow,
   Blow him again to me;
   While my little one, while my pretty one sleeps.

"Sleep and rest, sleep and rest,
   Father will come to thee soon;
   Rest, rest, on mother's breast,
   Father will come to thee soon;
   Father will come to his babe in the nest,
   Silver sails all out of the west
   Under the silver moon;
   Sleep my little one, sleep my pretty one, sleep."

After we finished, I put the harmonica down and closed my eyes. I felt little again. And happy. Like I was riding his shoulders home after a walk into the badlands.

Later that day Ma brought in my lunch tray. "Ah Sam wanted to thank you for all the music. He especially liked 'Sweet and Low,'" she said. "So he sent you this." She spread a bunch of knotted threads. There was a ship with silver sails.

"It's awfully pretty," I said.

"Where would you like me to hang it?" Ma asked.

I had thought Pirate Ursula was dead and gone, but I felt her stir and whisper, "Hang it near the bed so we can see it all the time."

I didn't want her back, though. Monster Ursula had to make a new life. "Just put it in a drawer," I said.

Ma was puzzled. "But why?"

I didn't want to explain. I just rolled over so she saw my back. "Because I don't feel like it," I said.

I thought about Ah Sam. I reckoned he wasn't so bad after all. Donkey people don't make silver-sailed boats.

"Would you tell him thank you and this is for him," I said to Ma.

I waited for a little bit so she could go into the kitchen and tell him. Then I began to play "Sweet and Low" again. I did it the best I could.

When I was finished, my curiosity bump began to itch something fierce. A present is a present, after all. So I went to my drawer and peeked at the string figure. Ah Sam had sent me a wish not in words but in knots. So I'd sent him a thank-you not in words but in musical notes. For the first time in a long time, I felt better.

The next day, Ma brought another string figure with lunch. "Ah Sam asked me what you would like, and I told him about Pirate Ursula. So he sent you something a sailor would see." She held it up. It was a fish woven from yellow silk thread.

I didn't reckon a fish could ever look so pretty, so I hung it up on the wall. Only it looked so lonesome that I got the boat out of the drawer and put it up beside the fish for company.

And then I sent him back a batch of toe-tapping tunes.

The next afternoon there was a pelican made from white thread. After that there was a dragon from green silk. Soon my room was full of cool, silky sea life. When a breeze from under the door brushed them, seabirds flew and dragons swam.

Sometimes I could almost pretend that the outside world had come into my room. Only it was better because I had never had dragons. And they would stay hidden with me at the Back of the Back of Beyond. I started to feel less lonesome.

I kept sending back tunes, and I always ended with "Sweet and Low." I began to think of Ah Sam as my far-away friend. Even though he was only as far as the kitchen, he might just as well have been in China.

Then one day Ah Sam sent me a complicated design of golden threads. "What is it?" I asked.

"Ah Sam says it's the Chinese word for happiness," Ma said.

It was hard to think of the pretty design as a word. It shone like a fine, bright spider's web. Maybe I could catch some happiness in it after all.

I hung it up because you could never have too much happiness. Especially now.

And at sunset the sun crept through the cracks above

the curtains. And the golden thread shone like treasure. It would have been part of Pirate Ursula's booty for sure.

I drew a picture to thank him. It started out as a ship with silver sails. But somehow Pirate Ursula took over. So it wound up being Pirate Ursula on her old ship with her bloodthirsty crew.

When I tried to give it to Ma to hand to him, Ma said, "I think it'd be nicer if you gave it to him yourself."

Suddenly I felt afraid. "I don't want to see anyone," I said.

"Ah Sam won't make fun of you," Ma insisted.

I was still scared. "But I'm so ugly."

Ma hugged me. "Sugar, you're only as ugly as you feel."

"Then why do folks laugh?" I demanded. "And why did Peter and Susie look at me so awful?"

"I've talked to them, and they really want to make it up to you," Ma said.

"Well, they can't," I said. "Not unless they can give me a new face."

When Ma left, I lay for a long time thinking about the world outside my room. Out there were all those folks who thought I was Monster Ursula. I studied my reflection in the mirror. Well, I reckoned they were right.

I tried to read a book, but I had read it a thousand times by now. I started to play my harmonica, but even that didn't help any.

I felt terribly restless. I just had to do something. So I got up and dressed. Then I took my scarf from the bureau and coiled it around my head. When it was good and tight, I checked my reflection. I couldn't see my cheeks. I could only see my eyes.

However, it was hard to breathe. So I tugged the scarf beneath my nose.

No one was in the dining room when I peeked. I snuck into the kitchen. Ah Sam was standing by a table cutting meat. He'd wound his queue around his neck like a snake. I guessed he didn't want it getting in the way.

Hanging from the wall were knives that looked like cleavers. Even their handles were metal. The edge of the one he was using must have been real sharp. It sliced through the bacon slab like it was sand. "Howdy-do," he said.

"How do you do," I said. "Where did you get those knives?"

"These are my knives," he said. "They're Chinese."

I thrust out the picture. "Here." I remembered to add, "Thank you for the string stuff."

He leaned forward and studied the picture. "That's very, very pretty."

Behind my scarf I frowned. "That's not pretty. That's Pirate Ursula and her bloodthirsty crew."

He raised his eyebrows. "What does a little girl know about pirates?"

So I told him what we had done last summer. And

27

with each story his eyebrows rose higher and higher. If they could have gone any farther, they would have been on top of his head.

"I don't think I'll sleep tonight," he said.

"Don't worry," I said. "Pirate Ursula's gone now."

I meant to leave, but Ah Sam nodded to a big can. "I got rice in there. Will you pound up about half a cup of it with water?"

It's funny. Just when I thought Pirate Ursula was dead and buried, her ghost popped up and whispered to me to see what was going to happen.

As he began to peel potatoes, Ah Sam supervised me. The first batch was too watery. So he had me pound more rice and add it. And then it got too thick, and I had to put in more water.

Eventually we wound up with a big bowl of paste. "That's sticky," I said.

"Rice sticks to your ribs," he said. "Now spread some on the back of the picture."

I got a knife and smeared it on the back of the picture. "Where do you want it?"

Ah Sam nodded to the wall near the stove. "Put it there. Then I can see it when I cook. It'll be just like a window."

When he had moved his head, his queue had unwound from his neck. The tip just touched the pan of potato peels.

After I had put up his picture, I lifted his queue out

of the pan. It felt like a thick, coarse rope. "Your hair's getting dirty," I said.

"Help me, please," he said, leaning his head to the side.

I carefully coiled it around his neck again. My curiosity bump acted up once more. "Why do you wear your hair so long?"

He frowned. "I don't want to. But the Manchus would kill me if I cut it."

"Who are the Manchus?" I asked.

"They are the barbarians who rule China," Ah Sam explained. "They make us wear our hair like horse tails. That reminds the Chinese of the horses the Manchus rode when they beat us."

"But you're here now," I said.

"But I want to go home someday," Ah Sam said. "I want to see my little girl."

I couldn't help asking, "How old is she?"

Ah Sam studied me from several angles and then said, "Just about your age."

"Did you make string animals for her, too?" I asked.

"I've never seen her," Ah Sam said. "I left before she was born."

"That's terrible," I said.

Ah Sam looked very solemn. "We lost three babies before we had our little girl. I'm just glad she's alive. She's why I'm here."

"But you've never seen her," I protested.

"I want to keep her alive," he said. "That's the most important thing. I just hope she's as pretty as you," Ah Sam said.

I couldn't help putting a hand to my cheeks. I felt the pit marks through the scarf. Once my face had been smooth. I thought Ah Sam was making fun of me. I got mad because I'd trusted him. "That's not a nice joke," I said, starting to leave.

"This is no joke," Ah Sam said. "Life is very precious. More precious than looks. If my dead babies were alive, I wouldn't care what they looked like."

My parents didn't care either. But then I remembered the donkey man. His big mouth had stretched so wide when he'd laughed at me. And Peter and Susie had been so horrified. "I just wish the rest of the world could think like that," I said.

"Your parents tell me in the old days you were outside all the time," Ah Sam said, picking up another potato. "Don't you miss that?"

Sometimes I thought I'd go crazy if I stayed inside anymore. But I fibbed, "No."

He placed the knife against the potato. His thumb was in back of the blade. "Too bad. I was hoping you could show me around. I like to walk. I used to walk all over when I was in China."

"And San Francisco too?" I asked. I would have liked

to hear about that city as well.

He shook his head sadly. "No, it was too dangerous there. Certain bad people like to beat up Chinese."

I felt right sorry about that. I would have liked to have shown him my own patch of America. And I would have if my face had been whole. "Is your home in China pretty?"

"Very pretty," he agreed. "But the animals were the best."

"So you could make the string figures?" I asked. "Did you see dragons there too?"

"No, not yet." As he pressed with his knife, the peel fell away in a long spiral. "My mother taught me how to make those and a lot of others. Then I learned to make more. When I go home, I'll make all sorts of things for my little girl. That way I'll show her all the wonderful things I saw in America."

Pirate Ursula began nudging me. "So when are you going back to China?"

"It's very far away, and it costs a lot of money to go there. My family is very poor, so I send money back to them." He dumped a peeled potato into a pot.

I didn't know what to say except "I'm sorry."

Ah Sam seemed awfully sad right then. He looked as lonely as I felt. Almost as if he were at the Back of the Back of Beyond too. "One day I'll save up enough money. Then I'll go home rich and see my daughter." He sighed. "Just like in your song. And my ship will have silver sails, too."

No wonder he liked "Sweet and Low." The song's words reminded him of himself and his own family.

Ah Sam got even sadder as he remembered his family in China. And it was my fault. I tried to change the subject. "What's China like?"

I was glad I'd asked that question. Ah Sam seemed happy to tell me about his valley and his fields. There were pines along the ridge top near the cemetery. I could almost smell the plum orchards in spring.

As he talked, he began to smile. It was like watching a candle light up inside a lantern. And I forgot about my face for a while. And I forgot about Monster Ursula.

I could even feel Pirate Ursula's ghost wanting to round up her crew and set sail for China.

It was just as well Ma came in before I did something stupid. There were piles of potato peels around our feet. They looked like long brown ribbons.

"Ursula, you're going to wear out poor Ah Sam," she scolded.

"Thank you," I said, remembering my manners.

"No, thank *you*," he said, and went back to peeling potatoes. "You can visit me anytime."

I went back to my room. In the dim light the animals were little blobs of color—like flowers on a foggy day.

Suddenly I didn't feel nearly as alone. I hoped Ah Sam felt the same way. I had a friend, and he wasn't far away anymore.

I had company at the Back of the Back of Beyond.

CHAPTER 5

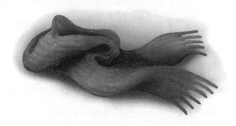

The Apprentice

Ah Sam had invited me to visit anytime. And Pirate Ursula's ghost kept trying to get me to go. But I reminded myself that I was Monster Ursula. And things always went wrong for Monster Ursula.

However, the loneliness started to ache inside. And it got so bad that even Monster Ursula couldn't take it. She'd have to leave the Back of the Back of Beyond again.

I wound my scarf around my head. Then I went looking for someone. But Ma and Pa were both busy. So I thought I'd try Ah Sam.

I poked my head into the kitchen and asked, "What are you up to?"

He set a bowl of eggs near the stove. "Getting ready for the stagecoach." Flour, bacon strips, spatulas and bowls were set up in even ranks like soldiers. Ah Sam looked like he was preparing for a battle.

"I'm sorry if I'm bothering you," I said, and started to leave.

"No, no, have a seat," he said, nodding to a chair.

I sat down and asked Ah Sam to tell me more about China. He seemed happy to talk about his home and family.

Suddenly I heard dogs begin to bark on the far side of town. The rattling thunder grew louder and louder until I could make out the thud of hooves and the rattle of wheels.

The stagecoach had come in. Inside would be people from Boston and New York, from San Francisco, from the Yukon, from Australia—from every place in the world. And our station fed them all.

The driver, Hank, bellowed, "Whoa, whoa." The thunder stopped, but the barking continued. "All out, ladies and gents."

I jumped to my feet. "I'd better go back to my room."

"Stay. I can talk while I cook," Ah Sam said.

Ma came rushing in. She grabbed an apron from a hook. "We must have a dozen passengers."

"I didn't think you could cram that many folks onto a stagecoach," I said as I helped tie the apron behind her.

"Some were on top and a couple sat with Hank. There's a ton of luggage and boxes, too," Ma said. "I'll have to give your pa a hand. You might have to cook as well as serve, Ah Sam."

Ah Sam picked up a frying pan in either hand. "Bring them on."

Ah Sam was like the captain of a ship caught in a storm. And I could hear Pirate Ursula whispering to me that I couldn't desert a friend in need.

"Can I help?" I finally asked. "I'll do anything but go out there." I nodded at the dining room.

Both of us wound up doing five things at the same time. When the passengers finally left, we collapsed on chairs in the kitchen and caught our breath.

It was only then that I saw my scarf on the kitchen floor. It lay there like a blue snake. Instinctively I clapped my hands to my pockmarked cheeks.

Ah Sam bent and leaned forward from his chair. Wiping his hands on his pants, he plucked the scarf from the floor. "With the fire roaring in the stove, I'm sweating. Isn't it too hot to wear that in here?" he asked.

I should have known that Ah Sam wasn't one of the donkey people. I could trust him as much as Ma and Pa. I wasn't Monster Ursula to them.

I lowered my hands and took the scarf. "I guess it is." And I draped my scarf over the back of the chair.

Later, as we cleaned up after the meal, I asked him, "Did you feel very lonely when you first came to America?"

"Very much," he replied. "At first I couldn't get work doing what I do best."

"Was that farming?" I asked.

"It doesn't matter. That's in the past." Ah Sam shrugged. "So I took a job in San Francisco as a houseboy to a family. I didn't even get to live in Chinatown."

"That's when you learned how to cook?" I asked.

"And speak English," he added. "I was so scared those first years." Ah Sam eyed me. "But you can't stay scared."

I tried to shrug. "It's different for other people."

"Why don't you show Whistle to me?" Ah Sam asked.

"Pa could show you better," I said.

"But you know what I like," he coaxed.

"I'll make out a list for Pa," I said.

Ah Sam kept at it so long that I finally got suspicious. "Did my parents put you up to this?"

He tilted his head back, offended. "I want to make new string animals for you."

I was tempted. But it meant leaving the station. "I don't go outside there anymore."

Ah Sam had thought about all my objections. "We can put on our hats. It's getting cool. You can wear your scarf outside too. No one will see you."

And Pirate Ursula whispered to me, "Why not?"

But Monster Ursula whispered back, "What if the scarf drops like it just did? And what if my friends see me and laugh? I'll just die."

"I don't want to talk about it anymore," I snapped at Ah Sam. "Tell me about China."

He arched an eyebrow. "Don't change the subject."

"I thought you liked talking about China," I said.

And over the clinking of dishes and cups, he began to tell me about his home again.

After that I started to help Ah Sam whenever a stagecoach came in. I would wind my scarf around my head so I could make the passage safely into the kitchen. But once I was there, I took it off.

I let Ma serve in the dining room. There was always plenty for me to do in the kitchen. Ah Sam even taught me how to use his Chinese kitchen knives. They sliced as well as American knives and chopped onions a lot better.

Ma and Pa started smiling again. "Even if Ah Sam's not the cook I am," Ma said, "he's been a big help. He's gotten Ursula out of her room."

I hadn't thought about that, but I guess he had.

Only he didn't stop there. It was his idea to promote me to assistant cook. I didn't want to at first. "Let me peel the potatoes and clean up the messes. I'll just burn everything."

"Of course you will. We all do," Ah Sam said. "But then you learn."

My first pancakes were more like lumps of coal and the bacon burnt. "Darn smoke," I said. "It's getting in my eyes." It was really the frustration, though. "You see? I told you it was a mistake."

He set down a bowl of fresh batter. "You try again."

Right then Ma hurried in with an empty pot of coffee. "Are those breakfasts ready yet? The passengers are starving." She started to wave her hand at the smoke. "Oh, did we have a fire?"

"No, it was just me," I said miserably.

"Please tell them breakfast will be worth the wait," Ah Sam said.

"But they have a schedule," I said. "You should do this batch."

"No one's perfect the first time or the next or the hundredth," Ah Sam scolded gently. "I still make plenty of mistakes. If your father were working in China with my little girl, I'd hope he'd tell her just what I'm telling you."

"But the stagecoach has to leave soon," I protested.

"The stagecoach won't leave without Hank, and Hank won't leave without his breakfast," Ma said to encourage me. "I'll explain things to him."

"What if Hank gets mad?" I asked, suddenly afraid.

If Ah Sam was the captain of his kitchen, Hank was the admiral of his stagecoach. Even Pa listened to Hank.

"Don't fret. He always asks about you," Ma said. "I'll tell him you're the one who's doing the cooking. He'll find a way to make up the lost time."

The second try was almost as bad, but you could at least eat the third attempt. Through the door I could hear a passenger grumble, "It's more ballast than food."

Hank, though, announced in a loud voice, "This is the best meal I ever ate." And all the complaints stopped. You didn't contradict Hank.

So for Hank's sake I'd keep at it until I made my pancakes almost as fluffy as Ah Sam's—though when I did, I wouldn't tell Ma.

It wasn't much, but it was something.

And maybe that was all Monster Ursula should expect.

CHAPTER 6

The Mark

Peter and Susie still kept coming by every day with my homework. When they did, they kept trying to apologize.

One day Susie said through the door, "I feel lower than the lowest skunk, Ursula. I didn't mean to hurt your feelings."

"I'm so clumsy that folks laugh at me all the time," Peter added. That was the straight truth, but I had more manners than him and hadn't made fun of him.

"I just wish you'd quit pestering me," I told them.

When I was sure they'd gone, I opened my door to get my homework. Ah Sam was standing in the kitchen doorway, looking thoughtful. "Are those your friends?"

"A long time ago," I said.

"Am I your friend now?" he asked.

"Sure." I shrugged.

He folded his arms. "Well, what if you show Whistle to your friend?"

My stomach did flip-flops. "I can't."

His fingers twitched. "But my hands want to make something."

"Make me another dragon," I suggested.

"I'm tired of dragons." He shrugged. His hand dove into his basket and he took out some thread. "I'm going to try to make an elephant." He added, "But it might not look very good. I have to do this from memory."

"You've seen an elephant?" I asked in amazement.

"He was in an American circus," Ah Sam said. "My former employers asked me to take their children to one in San Francisco."

I'd wanted to see a circus more than anything. "I've only read about circuses. Were there clowns?" I asked eagerly.

He nodded. "Plenty of clowns."

"And acrobats?" I asked.

"Lots of those," he said. "But they aren't as good as Chinese ones."

"And lions?" I asked wistfully.

"Only one," he said, "but it was a big one."

"Was it . . . ?" I hunted for the right word. "Was it magic?" There wasn't any of that in my life anymore.

"Yes, very magical," he decided.

"I wish I could have seen it"—I sighed—"especially

the animals. I wish I could have seen that circus more than anything else." There was magic at the circus—unlike Whistle now that Pirate Ursula was gone.

He studied me. "I think there's an American circus coming into the city next spring. I bet your parents would take you," he said.

It would be nice to see some magic again. I felt Pirate Ursula's ghost stir and whisper to me, "What are you waiting for? Let's go!"

However, I remembered what Pa had said. City folk were rude. They were probably all donkey people.

Pirate Ursula was persistent, though. She whispered to me, "I bet Cutthroat Peter and Killer Susie would go if we did."

They weren't monsters.

Reluctantly I shook my head. "I just don't go outside," I insisted to Ah Sam.

"Then I'll do my best to bring it to you," Ah Sam said gently. A week later, I had an elephant made out of silver string.

Almost every day he had some new string animal for my "circus." My parents started talking about going to the city to see the real circus. I reckoned Ah Sam must have talked to them.

I was mightily tempted. Pirate Ursula kept telling me that this was my chance to see the magic. But I always thought about a tent full of strangers. Would they laugh at clowns? Or would they laugh at me instead?

The circus was like Pirate Ursula. They belonged to my old life. The life before I got trapped at the Back of the Back of Beyond. As much as it hurt inside, I had to shut the door on all that. And on the magic, too. It was hard, though, to think of a life without any magic.

"I don't want to ever hear about the circus again," I told everyone.

Even though they gave up talking about the circus, Ma and Pa and Ah Sam kept trying to get me to leave the station.

Round about November, Ma got real serious. I was peeling potatoes with her in the kitchen when she said, "You know, Ursula, you can't stay holed up in your room forever."

I got scared. I didn't want to think about the future. "You wouldn't kick me out, would you?" I asked.

Ma stroked my hair. "Course not, Sugar. But your pa and I won't always be here."

That scared me even more. "Then I hope I die before you." I could feel the tears begin to sting my eyes.

Ma hugged me. "Shh, Sugar. Shh. I'm sorry." When I had calmed down, Ma asked. "Did I ever tell you about Louisa? She was my best friend when I was your age."

Ma didn't talk about her childhood much. It had sounded pretty rough.

"Was she as good a friend as Susie?" I asked.

"Yes," Ma said. "She was the kindest person you'd ever meet, but she had a harelip. That means she was born with a split right here." Ma touched her upper lip. "There were donkey people who made fun of her. But you couldn't have found a kinder person or a better friend."

"What did she do when people laughed at her?" I asked.

"She cried," Ma admitted. "But there were people who could see what she was like inside. Eventually she married one of them. Last I heard, she was a mother of four. And luckier children I couldn't think of."

I was glad for Louisa, but that didn't make me feel any better personally. "That's nice," I said carefully.

Ma cleared her throat. "She didn't stew in her own misery, if you know what I mean."

I knew Ma was trying to tell me to follow Louisa's example. I really wanted to, but right now it was like asking me to fly. "I'm not like her, Ma. I'm sorry," I said. Her story only made me feel even more helpless and frustrated.

Suddenly we heard Pa outside. "That's a nice piece of venison, Tom!"

Tom was a real Sioux who lived up in the hills. "Thought you might want to buy it."

I peeked out through the curtain. Tom was tall and dark. On his head was a battered old hat, and he wore a flannel shirt and denims. He was holding the venison up for Pa to see. Over his shoulder was a bloody sack. Ma was curious too, so she pressed up behind me. Maybe I'd gotten my curiosity bump from her.

"I heard you got a Chinese working for you," Tom said.

"He's a fine cook," Pa boasted. Luckily, he remembered in time. "Almost as good as my wife."

"Isn't that like two men?" Ma clicked her tongue. "Blood dripping all over the floor." She hurried through the doorway. "Howdy, Tom. Let me take that into the kitchen."

Ma fetched the side of deer and hung it out back. Then she cleaned the floor while Pa and Tom began to chat about the hunting up in the hills. "You should come up sometime. We'll get some wild birds for your table," Tom said.

Even when I had been Pirate Ursula, the Scourge of the Seven Seas, I had not been keen about hunting. Don't get me wrong—I liked meat. I just didn't like to think how it got to my plate. Hunting, though, was what almost everyone did up here.

When Ma came back into the kitchen, she nudged me. "Don't you want to come outside and say hello to Tom?"

My curiosity bump was itching worse than ten mosquito bites. However, I shook my head. "I can't."

Before Ma could work on me anymore, we heard the distant thunder. In the dining room Pa stopped talking to Tom. "Stagecoach coming in. Excuse me, Tom. You set right there, and we'll settle up when the coach is gone. Meantime, you can sample our cook's work."

We all had to hop to it then, because passengers just

47

kept pouring through the door. I don't know how Hank packed them into the stagecoach. He must have stacked them on the roof like firewood.

We fed them all, though, including Tom. Suddenly, Ah Sam slapped his forehead. "My letter." Though he wrote the address in English, his letters were always in Chinese to his family back home. He picked up an envelope from a table. "I almost forgot to give this to Hank."

He hurried out of the kitchen into the dining room. The next moment I heard a crash. When I peeked out through the door, I saw Ah Sam on the floor. A bald man was still in his chair, but his leg was stretched out. I figured he must have tripped Ah Sam.

"Chinaman," the man said, "you ought to say, 'Excuse me.'" He had the mean grin all bullies have.

Ah Sam glared up at the man. At first I thought he was going to get up and punch the man, but Ah Sam said, "Excuse me."

The bald man turned to a woman. "I told you Chinamen were all cowards. That's why their skin's yellow." He started to laugh and slap the table at his own joke.

When Ah Sam got up, I saw he was shaking. It wasn't from fear, though. It was anger.

Then Hank rumbled from his table, "You numbskull. He can't hit back no matter how much he wants to. There's parts of this state where it'd be worth his neck to strike a white man—no matter how much he should."

I felt ashamed because I'd also been thinking that

Ah Sam had no courage. I wanted to rush out there and tell that man what I thought of him. But the bald man would have turned his attention to me. If anyone was a coward, it was me.

Fortunately Hank got up. "On the other hand, I'm free to hit who I like."

The bald man knew better than to pick a fight with Hank. Even if Hank hadn't been the stagecoach driver, he was a head taller.

The bald man swung around and pretended to interest himself in his cup of coffee. "Let's forget it." He shrugged.

Hank glared at him. "I got a good mind to let you walk the rest of the way."

Ah Sam managed to keep his voice steady as he held the letter out to Hank. "Would you mail this?" he asked.

Hank stooped and picked it up. "I'll put it in the mail pouch."

"Thank you," Ah Sam said.

Then Hank told everyone to finish up because it was time to leave. With Hank riding herd, the passengers cleared out of the station for the stagecoach again.

"I'm so sorry," Ma said right away.

"It happens." Ah Sam shrugged.

"I heard about you," said Tom as he got up.

"Where are my manners?" exclaimed Ma. "Tom, this is our cook, Ah Sam. Ah Sam, this is Tom," Ma said, making the introductions.

Though Ah Sam couldn't have felt much like it, he nodded politely. "Howdy-do."

Tom strode over and gazed at Ah Sam. "You got the mark, all right."

Ah Sam pointed at a mole on the back of his left hand. "You mean this?"

Tom stroked the back of his arm. "I mean this." He touched his face. "And this."

"This what?" Ah Sam asked, puzzled.

Tom grabbed Ah Sam's wrist and held his own hand up against the cook's. "We got the same skin. The same eyes. That's the mark."

"The mark of what?" Ah Sam asked, even more puzzled.

"We're the ones standing outside looking at the party inside," said Tom.

"But you're always welcome here," Ma said in distress.

Tom grinned. "I know that, but there's a lot of folks who see it otherwise."

And then he left with Ma to get his money.

I didn't understand what Tom meant by "the mark." I figured he was just talking funny. Maybe he'd gotten a little touched sitting on his hill.

Ah Sam didn't say anything when he came through the doorway. He just headed for his cot in the corner. When he lay down, he curled up on his side and faced the wall.

I gave a start. I lay in my bed the same way sometimes.

That bald man couldn't see past Ah Sam's skin. Just like some donkey people hadn't seen past the harelip of Ma's friend Louisa. Or just like my Swiss cheese face. Maybe that's what Tom meant about "the mark."

And I had thought Ah Sam and I were just friends because we were both stuck at the Back of the Back of Beyond. But now I realized there were plenty of us—me and him and Tom and Louisa.

"Ah Sam—" I began.

"I don't want to talk," he said without looking at me.

I thought of all the words I wanted to say to comfort him. But I didn't say them. They hadn't made things right for me. They wouldn't make things right for him either.

CHAPTER 7

The Christmas Debt

The rest of November, I tried to talk to Ah Sam about "the mark." I wanted to tell him that I understood now. He wasn't alone here. He had someone who also knew about the donkey people.

However, Ah Sam always changed the subject. When I asked Ma about that, she said he was probably still mad and ashamed of not fighting the bully. "It takes a strong person to do what he *has* to do, and not what he *wants* to do."

So I thought of another way to tell Ah Sam that I felt close to him. I started to draw pictures for his daughter. He always gave me a big smile and sent each picture off in his next letter.

Still, it wasn't much. I kept trying to think of other

things I could do for him, but I wasn't coming up with a lot of ideas.

By late November the air got really chilly. We started to spend all our spare time in the kitchen, since Ah Sam had a fire going in the stove most of the day and night.

When Pa came in from the stables, he was so cold he kept his coat on. As he sipped his mug of tea, he said, "The horses are already growing long coats. It's going to be a hard winter. I'd better order extra hay."

"The snow can't be far off," I said. I thought of all the games Pirate Ursula could have organized for her crew. We could have ridden polar bears and chased Deadly Dan.

Ah Sam saw how sad I was.

"How about some hot chocolate?" he asked kindly.

We had the first snow two days later. Susie and Peter came around to ask me to play. I told Ma to tell them no.

Inside my bedroom I could hear them laughing outside. When I peeked, I saw they were throwing snowballs. Susie was better at dodging than Peter. Peter squealed the loudest whenever Susie hit him with a snowball.

Suddenly Susie saw me. "Ursula!"

I closed the curtain quick, but not quick enough.

"Pirate Ursula, your crew misses you," Peter complained.

"The games aren't any fun without you," Susie added. "No one has your imagination."

They begged me to talk to them, but I hunkered down and wouldn't budge.

Finally they gave up. I heard them talking as they moved off. My hand pressed the curtain against the window so I could feel their voices vibrating in the glass. That's the way life is for monsters.

The days got darker and colder. Everyone clumped around the station as if they were at the Back of the Back of Beyond too. Pa said he was so busy that we wouldn't have time to decorate a tree this year, so he wasn't going to bother to get one. Ma had lots of things to do too. She said maybe we wouldn't worry about presents either. And I didn't argue. Monsters don't celebrate Christmas.

It got so cold that Pa and Ma really had to bundle up whenever they went outside. It was funny, though: Ah Sam still wore only his cotton shirt and pants and thin cloth shoes.

At first I thought it was because he didn't feel the cold.

Then one day he went out to the woodpile to collect logs to feed the stove. When he came back in, his teeth were chattering.

He dropped the logs by the stove. His hand shook so badly when he tried to pick up the kettle of hot water that it spilled all around the cup instead of inside it.

"Let me pour," I said. I wrapped a rag around my hand and picked up the hot metal handle of the kettle.

When I had filled the cup, Ah Sam didn't drink the

water at first. Instead, he kept his hands wrapped around the cup for warmth.

"You should wear your coat," I said.

"I don't have one," he said, sipping the steaming water. "I never needed one in San Francisco."

"Why don't you buy one then?" I asked, puzzled.

"If I get a coat, I have less money to send home." He shrugged.

I was so ashamed that I felt like crawling into a hole. I thought of all his many kindnesses. Life wouldn't have been the same without him. Ah Sam was family.

I thought of what he had said to me when he was giving me cooking lessons. Well, what if Pa were working in China and he were freezing there? Wouldn't I want some little girl to help him somehow?

And then I thought about Christmas. There wasn't a better holiday to help someone.

I hadn't been looking forward to Christmas. Now I had a warm feeling inside.

I corralled my folks and told them about Ah Sam.

Pa sighed. "Well, Sugar, he has the right to spend his money the way he wants."

When it came to organizing, I still had all my old pirate skills. "But he'll get frostbit," I said, "or worse. And then it'll be our fault. Can't we give him some old clothes?"

Ma thought about it. "Your pa's old coat is just lying around in our trunk. He never wears it anymore."

Pa snapped his fingers. "And Ah Sam's small, so I

bet a pair of your old boots might fit him."

"Ma, if you help me, I'll knit him something," I suggested.

Pa walked over and got his hat from a peg. "While you round up the gear, I'll get the tree."

"But you said you were too busy," Ma said.

"A present looks awfully lonesome without a tree," Pa said.

Ma smiled. "Well, maybe we ought to have other gifts to keep it company."

Pa took a buckboard and went out to round up a tree. It took him most of a day to find the perfect tree and chop it down and bring it back. But when he did, didn't the station smell nice? Usually at this time of year the passengers were cold and tired and grumpy from the trip. However, they got right cheery as soon as they saw the tree.

As I worked at my gifts, that warm feeling inside me kept getting warmer and brighter. Helping out Ah Sam made me forget about my own problems.

And the closer it got to Christmas, the warmer and toastier I felt inside. It was the best Christmas feeling that I'd ever had.

It only got hard when my friends came caroling. They stopped by our house. Peter was off-key as usual. If I'd been there, I could have nudged him back in tune with my elbow.

I wanted to go outside real bad. Instead, I lay down on my bed and covered my head with my pillow. But I could still hear them. They all sounded happy. It didn't seem fair.

Then I felt ashamed of myself. After all, Christmas wasn't about being selfish. It was about helping others. I had to think of Ah Sam and not about myself. I picked up my knitting again.

Ma came inside with a plate of cookies. "Don't you want to give these to your friends, Ursula?" she asked.

My needles went even faster. *Click. Click. Click.*

Why couldn't Ma leave me alone? Even if things were nicer at the Back of the Back of Beyond, I was still Monster Ursula.

"I'm sorry, but I'm very busy," I said.

So Ma took them outside instead. "This is more treasure stolen by Pirate Ursula," she said.

Ma didn't realize the game was over.

Neither did Peter or Susie.

"Thank you, Pirate Ursula," Peter said.

"Thanks, Captain," Susie called.

"Pirate Ursula's still dead," I whispered.

Click, click, click went the needles.

I felt tears in my eyes. I wiped them away with the back of my hand. Then I went back to knitting. Instead of feeling sorry for myself, I pictured Ah Sam's face when we gave him warm winter clothes.

All that week before Christmas the excitement grew and grew inside me like a bubble. By Christmas Eve I thought I was going to explode. I kept thinking about how surprised and happy Ah Sam would be.

When Christmas finally came, Ma and Pa seemed just as excited. Inside his kitchen, Ah Sam also sang—though it was some Chinese tune and not a Christmas carol.

For supper Ah Sam marched out of his kitchen, beaming with pleasure. "Just like in a fancy San Francisco restaurant," he declared.

And he set down a wild partridge with stuffing.

Pa leaned forward and sniffed. Then he closed his eyes in happiness. It certainly smelled heavenly.

"Where did you get the bird?" he asked.

"From Tom," Ah Sam said. "I know Christmas is important to you. I wanted to serve something special."

Pa gestured toward a chair. "Won't you sit and share the feast with us?"

Ah Sam hesitated. "It's yours. I cooked food for myself."

"There's plenty for everyone," Ma insisted.

"Well . . ." Ah Sam scratched his head uncomfortably.

"Is there something wrong?" I asked, worried.

He looked embarrassed. "Could I have rice?"

Pa sampled the bread stuffing. "But this is delicious."

"It's not a real meal without rice," Ah Sam insisted.

"Whatever it takes to get you to the table." Pa grinned and pulled out a chair for him.

So Ah Sam brought out a bowl of rice and chopsticks.

He would cut the meat on his plate and then switch to chopsticks and eat it with his rice.

When everyone was stuffed, my parents excused themselves.

Ah Sam started to get up to clear the table, but I grabbed his arm.

"You stay right there," I ordered, and ran into my room to fetch the presents.

Pa got a new pipe from Ma and me. Ma got a new shawl from Pa and me. I got a new book from my parents. It was *The General History of the Robberies and Murders of the Most Notorious Pirates* by Daniel Defoe.

"We thought it would give you ideas for your games," Ma explained.

"Huzzah!" Pirate Ursula said to me. "And no quarter!"

I wished Pirate Ursula would realize she was only a ghost and not bother me. But out loud I said, "Thank you." At least it was nice to have something new to read.

Ah Sam politely admired everything. "Now I'll wash up," he said.

"Not yet." I handed a burlap bag with a ribbon to Ah Sam.

When he hauled out the coat and boots, he sat back in amazement and just stared.

"There's more," I said, poking him in the ribs.

When he took out the mittens, cap and scarf I had

knitted, he just stroked them like they were soft kittens. "All of this is for me?" When we assured him it was, he had to try them on right then and there.

The boots were fine, but the coat was too big. So was the cap, which came down over his eyes. Ah Sam didn't seem to care.

He rolled the cap brim up to his forehead and wound the scarf around his face. "I feel like a stove in my winter clothes," he said through his scarf.

"Now you can stay warm when you go outside," I said.

When he unwound the scarf from his face, though, he looked real sad.

That was the last expression I had imagined he would have.

So I nudged him. "You're supposed to be happy. What's wrong? Don't you like your presents?"

"I love them, but we Chinese don't celebrate Christmas," he said. "I've got no gifts for you."

I shrugged and smiled. "It's okay. That's not the point to Christmas."

However, I hadn't realized how proud a man Ah Sam was. He tilted back his head. "What would you most like, Ursula?"

"A new face," I said automatically.

"Ursula." Ma sighed.

"Besides that?" asked Ah Sam.

I wished he hadn't brought it up. For a little while I'd forgotten about my Swiss cheese face, and I'd been happy. "There's nothing else," I said sadly.

He smiled slyly. "No, I think I know another wish."

"I ought to know my own mind," I retorted.

"Maybe yes, maybe no," he said. Still wearing all his winter finery, Ah Sam clomped around as he cleared the table.

The next day when the stagecoach came, we fed all the passengers. Then Ah Sam picked up a letter and left the kitchen.

"Wonderful meal, Ah Sam," said Hank.

"Please take good care of this letter," Ah Sam requested.

"Another letter home?" asked Hank. "No, this says to San Francisco." Hank was nice, but he was also very nosy.

"This is for my cousins. They're in this country, but they're traveling around," Ah Sam explained. "These people will know where they are."

Hank tucked the letter inside his coat. "For the best cook in the state, I'll guard it like gold," promised Hank.

I figured Ah Sam was asking his cousins for something for me. I hoped it was one of those painted fans I'd read about in the newspapers, but it could be something else.

My curiosity bump was itching something fierce now.

CHAPTER 8

The Three Bears

January came and went and still no present. My curiosity bump swelled to the size of a hill. And did it ever itch!

Every day I asked Ah Sam for hints. And every day he just smiled. "You'll see when it comes," he would say. That would have been bad enough, but then he would add, "You're really going to like it, though."

He was lucky he was my friend, or I would have turned Pirate Ursula loose long enough to keelhaul him.

In early February I slipped into the kitchen. The stagecoach was due, and I wanted to help him.

Ah Sam was wearing all his Christmas presents. "Put on your coat so we can go outside," he told me.

I shook my head annoyed. "I don't go out anymore. Don't you know that by now?"

Ah Sam shrugged. "Too bad."

He clomped out of the kitchen and into the dining room.

I raced into my bedroom and peeked through the curtains. Ah Sam marched out into the street. He stood beside Pa.

It was even too cold for the dogs to bark, so all I heard was the rattling thunder of the stagecoach. When it rolled to a stop in front of the station, it was loaded down with trunks and boxes. I figured a pile that big must belong to at least a half dozen passengers.

However, only three people got off. In their long coats and caps they looked round as bears. There was a big one, a medium one and a baby one.

Ah Sam greeted them in Chinese. Then he looked inside the stagecoach for someone else. When he didn't see anyone, he turned back and spoke to the three bears. This time his voice sounded more urgent.

They just held up their hands.

Ah Sam looked bothered as he helped Pa haul all the trunks and boxes off the stagecoach. I didn't think three people could own that many clothes.

When they came inside the station, I opened my door a crack. In the dining room the three bears peeled off their coats. Then they took off layer after layer of sweaters. Finally all that was left was a thin Chinese man and woman and boy.

Ah Sam introduced them to my parents. "These are

my cousins." He motioned to Papa Bear. "This is Ah Bing." Mama Bear was Ah Loo, and Baby Bear was Lung.

Pa shook their hands. "Pleased to meet you," he said.

Ah Sam beamed. "My cousins would like to meet Ursula. Then, in six days we'll go up to the city to the Chinatown. We'll celebrate Chinese New Year's there. Is that all right?" Ah Sam asked Pa.

"But we already had New Year's," said Ma.

"The Chinese use a different calendar," Ah Sam explained.

Ma and Pa exchanged looks. Finally Ma shrugged so Pa said, "There aren't many folks traveling in this season. I don't see why you shouldn't have a holiday," said Pa.

Ah Sam had a cot in the kitchen, but there wasn't enough room for his cousins too.

Ma waved a hand at the big tables in the dining room. "I guess we could rig some beds on top there."

Ah Sam turned toward my door. "My cousins would really like to meet Ursula," he repeated.

I shut my door quickly. Why did he have to say something like that? He knew how I felt about strangers. I was feeling awfully hurt, so I went over and plopped down on my bed.

Of course, Ma came in the next moment. I knew she would. "Won't you say hello to Ah Sam's cousins?" she coaxed.

I clung to my pillow. "I don't want to."

"They traveled a long way just to see you," Ma reminded me.

I felt real guilty. That made them my guests in a way. "But what if they laugh?"

Ma got my long scarf from my bureau. "They won't if they're Ah Sam's kin. But you can always wear this."

If they were Ah Sam's family, they had the mark too. So I coiled the scarf around my head.

Then Ma patted me on the back. "Let's go meet our company."

Ah Sam smiled when I came into the dining room. His cousins didn't seem surprised to see my face covered. I guess he had told them about me.

They nodded their heads. "Hello," said Ah Bing.

"Hello," I said timidly. "Thank you for coming all this way."

"Ah Sam say you friends," said Ah Bing. His English wasn't as good as his cousin's. "You want see circus."

I shot an annoyed look at Ah Sam. Had he told them all my secrets? "I don't go outside anymore," I explained sullenly. "I've been sick."

Ah Bing spread his arms out wide. "We know. So we bring circus to you."

Ah Sam waved his hand proudly at his cousins. "They came from China to put on shows here. In two days they will put on a circus in the street. First, though, they need to practice a new trick. You invite the whole town for Saturday."

I gave a snort. This sounded like some practical joke. "No offense meant, but just the three of them?"

Ah Sam stared at me. "What do you think a circus is? Big tents and big bands and lots of performers?"

I scratched my head. "Well, isn't it?"

Ah Sam shook his head. "The magic doesn't come from size and flash."

I knew better than that though. There was no such thing as magic anymore. "Well, where does it come from?" I demanded skeptically.

"From inside," Ah Sam replied, and pointed. "From inside something like that bench or that cup or my boot."

"I don't see how," I snorted.

"Just you wait. There'll be clowns and acrobats," Ah Sam promised.

"Well, there won't be animals," I said. "A circus has got to have animals."

Ah Sam winked. "There'll be one, anyway."

I folded my arms stubbornly. "Whatever show you put on, it's got to be outside my window."

"Don't you want to sit right in front?" Ah Sam asked in disappointment.

I shook my head so hard I almost loosened my scarf. Afraid, I held it up against my face. "You know why."

"We'll do it then." Ah Sam sighed.

"I'll keep you company in here," Ma promised me.

Ah Sam scratched his head. "My cousins have a problem. My other cousin couldn't make it. He plays the music." I guess that was why he had been so upset when he had met the stagecoach.

"It would have been nice to hear Chinese music, but that's okay," I said. "Where are you keeping the animal?"

"You'll see in good time. Now if you'll excuse us. They have to rehearse. It's tricky without music," said Ah Sam. "May we practice in here?"

"Why not?" Pa beamed. He was as happy as a small boy. "If we get any passengers, they'll just have to eat in the corners."

"We'll need blankets and clothesline," said Ah Sam.

"We do new trick," Ah Bing said. "No one must see."

With Pa's help they moved the tables. Then they strung up clothesline and hung up blankets.

By the time they were done, my curiosity bump was the size of a mountain. Ah Sam knew that by now. He made a point of wagging an index finger at me. "No peeking, Ursula. The trick is for you."

Ma put her hands on my shoulders. "Ursula wouldn't spoil her own surprise."

I'd been thinking to do just that. I started to blush. Behind the scarf I felt like I was in a furnace.

"Curses," whispered Pirate Ursula in annoyance.

Pa was buttoning up his coat again. "Well, I'd better be spreading the news."

"I'll help," said Ma, getting her coat. Then she gave me a gentle pat on the backside. "Scoot into your bedroom now, Ursula."

"I didn't do anything bad," I harumphed, but I went inside.

When my parents left, though, I opened my door a crack. From behind the blankets came lots of thumping and grunting. Lots of thuds, too.

The next two days I hardly ever saw Ah Sam's cousins. All I heard were strange noises from behind the curtains.

The night before the circus, I hardly slept. I hadn't been so excited since Pirate Ursula had been born.

I woke up before sunrise. So I heard the noise in the street. When I peeked out, I saw John from the Circle-T ranch. His family rode on a buckboard while all the cowboys trotted behind them. Word must have spread out there somehow.

As he passed my window, John gave the secret pirate sign for hello.

Shortly afterward tall Tom came in on snowshoes. He must have walked all night down from his hills.

Then I heard a loud *shoosh-shoosh* sound. It was the miners on skis they had made themselves. Even they had quit work and left their coal mine. Harry rode on his father's shoulders. He gave me the secret greeting too.

The whole pirate crew arrived for the circus. In fact, the whole town shut down. Mr. Schultz, Peter's father, came out of his barber shop with a shovel. As he started to clear the snow off the street, Pa got his shovel and joined him. Soon there were a dozen people working. Snow fountained up on either side like a tail of white plumes.

When that was done, people piled up logs and old lumber and crates. Soon flames roared upward. Everyone gathered around the bonfire to keep warm.

Then I heard the front door slam. "Everything's ready," Pa announced excitedly. His lower lip was all swollen, though.

"What happened to your mouth?" asked Ma.

"Oh, that old shovel handle reared up and hit me in the face," Pa said.

I put my scarf around my face and went out into the dining room. Ma was waiting to see Ah Sam and the three bears off.

Ah Sam came out from behind the blankets in his regular Christmas clothes. However, his cousins wore satin costumes of red and blue with designs in gold thread. I felt like parrots had landed in my home.

"Don't forget. You're supposed to do it in front of my window," I reminded him anxiously.

Ah Sam didn't look happy. "We've tried and tried our routines without music. But they don't work. My cousins count on songs to get the right rhythm."

"Just try your best," I told his cousins. "No one will know the difference."

71

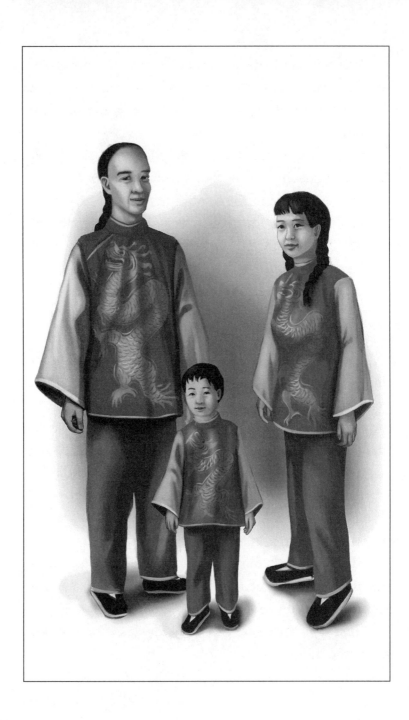

Ah Bing lifted his head proudly. "But we will know. We cannot do."

"Won't you play your harmonica for us, Ursula?" asked Ah Sam.

My stomach did flip-flops again. "Pa could."

Pa touched his swollen lip. "Not with this."

My worst nightmare was rearing up to bite me. "I don't go outside," I insisted. "I'm going to watch from the window."

Ah Sam suddenly spread his arms. "I got an idea. What if we sneak you out when no one's looking? You can stand behind the crowd."

I shook my head. "Nope."

Ah Sam sighed. "Then we'll just have to call off the circus."

"Oh, dear," said Mama. "Everybody will be so disappointed."

"They'll just have to understand." Pa shrugged.

"I don't go outside," I snapped.

But then I thought of all the people outside. I thought of Peter and Susie and all my old pirate crew. I thought of the cowboys from their ranch and Tom from his hill far away and the miners from their mountain. I could just imagine their sad faces. Pa looked the most disappointed of all.

That almost broke my heart. "Are you sure everybody will be watching the circus?"

"I promise," said Ah Sam.

"All right," I mumbled, "but if any head turns toward me, I scoot right back inside."

"Thank you," said Ah Bing.

Ma commenced to fret then about our guests' thin costumes. "Aren't you going to be cold outside?"

"We move around. Keep warm," Ah Bing assured her. "Now that Ursula help us."

I wish I could have been as sure as he was about me. "I don't know how much help I'll be."

"You'll do just fine," Ah Sam whispered.

He didn't have a crystal ball, though. And if I'd had one right then, I would have read doom, gloom and the End of the World for sure.

CHAPTER 9

The Circus

In my bedroom my fingers were trembling so much,
I had a hard time putting on my coat and boots. I
wrapped the scarf around my face real careful again.

When I went back into the dining room, Ma was
already dressed for outside.

Nervously I asked Ah Sam, "What should I play?"

He checked with his cousins and then told me, "Anything fast and lively."

While Ah Sam's cousins marched outside, I was
feeling so scared that my tummy did flip-flops like an
acrobat. Then everyone started to clap. It sounded like a
thunderstorm had fallen onto my street. And I felt like
my stomach was putting on a whole circus of its own.

While they were bowing, Mama poked me and
whispered, "I think it's okay."

I nudged her back. "You go first, and make sure."

She stepped outside and then nodded. "No one's looking."

The cold air hit my face. It stole my breath. The sweet, fresh air smelled good, though. I hadn't been outside in a long time. Overhead, the big sky stretched like a gray, pebbly road.

Quiet as a mouse, I tiptoed behind the crowd. Ah Sam took his place at the side. When he raised his hand, I glanced around. No one was watching me.

I took a deep breath and pulled down my scarf. Putting the harmonica to my lips, I started to play "Tramp! Tramp! Tramp! The Boys Are Marching."

With a hop and a skip Ah Sam's cousins began to bounce around like human balls.

"They look like they're made of rubber," Susie said out loud in wonder.

They twisted their bodies into hoops and rolled around the street. Lung even slipped right through Ah Bing's circle.

In the meantime Ah Sam brought out a whole bunch of small benches. I didn't pay them much mind because they looked so ordinary. I figured they were for the audience, who were all standing.

While Lung disappeared inside the station, Ah Sam swung the benches in front of the crowd.

Before anyone could sit on any of them, though, Ah Bing lay down on his back on one of them. Then he stuck his feet in the air like a dead beetle.

As Ah Sam handed her the benches, Ah Loo began to build a pyramid of benches on top of Ah Bing's feet and climb up it. Higher and higher went the pyramid. Higher and higher went Ah Loo. Finally she was as high as the tallest building. Everyone had to lean far back to look up at her as she twirled and spun, graceful as a spider on a thread.

To me, getting down seemed trickier than going up. However, Ah Loo neatly took apart the pyramid as she climbed down.

While Mama and Papa caught their breath, Ah Sam quickly turned the benches into ramps and tables. Then Lung rolled out of our station on a unicycle, cycling up and down, quick and nimble as a flea. He did better on one wheel than I could have done running on two legs. And it was all on ordinary benches.

Everybody craned their heads to look when Ah Sam came out of the station with a basket of small balls and a sword as long as my arm.

"Aw, I bet that sword isn't sharp," called Peter from the front row.

"Go ahead and touch one," Ah Sam said, "but be careful."

Naturally Peter put his finger against the tip. "Ow." He snatched his finger back. When Ah Sam had tied up his finger in a clean rag, he warned everyone, "Now, my cousin knows what she's doing. Don't any of you children try this." He looked right at Peter.

Ah Loo commenced to swallow some balls, spitting them out and catching them again like she was a fountain. Then she took the sword and held it over her head with the point aimed at her mouth. I didn't think she'd get more than the tip inside. I got so excited that I forgot to breathe.

Hurriedly Ah Sam waved his arm at me. Some orchestra I was! I began blowing "Sweet Betsy from Pike" on my harmonica.

Slowly, inch by inch, Ah Loo lowered that sword into her mouth. I thought she'd cut up her insides something awful, but she slid the sword back out with a smile.

As everyone clapped, Ah Sam lit a couple of torches from the bonfire. Then he presented them to her like a bouquet. And pretty as you please, she commenced to dine on them daintily. You would have thought she was having her daily snack. And for her main course, Ah Loo ate fire and spat it out from her mouth.

As she skipped into the station, we heard enough clanging and clatter to wake the dead. I thought a locomotive was chugging through it.

It was Ah Bing. He waddled out in an apron with his arms full of pots and pans.

Cheerfully he went right up to Susie. Putting a hand behind her ear, he plucked out an egg. He held it up to everyone as we started to laugh. Quickly he scampered around the audience, gathering eggs from people. The biggest one came from the beard of Mr. Schultz, Peter's father. Mr. Schultz laughed the loudest of anyone. Ah Bing might not be dressed up like a regular clown, but he was just as funny.

However, when Ah Bing cooked the eggs, his meal turned out all wrong. As things got worse and worse, people laughed harder and harder. I got a little scared when a pot caught on fire. But when Ah Bing raised the lid, the flames had changed into bright red and yellow flowers.

By now I had played every tune I knew, and I knew lots of them. So I started over with "Battle Hymn of the Republic."

Ah Sam took off his winter clothes. Underneath, he was decked out in an outfit just like his cousins. It was such an outlandish outfit that my jaw dropped open and I stopped playing.

"Why are you in that getup?" Susie cried out.

Ah Sam gave a little bow. Then he announced, "In China I was in a circus too. But then I retired and came to America. I went to work as a houseboy. However, today, for you, I will do my act."

I blinked. I saw Ah Sam's face on top of a parrot costume. He had changed from a cook and my friend to a juggler. Maybe there was magic after all—circus magic.

From his bag Ah Sam hauled out all his big Chinese kitchen knives and some cups and balls, just as a wind roared into town. It drove the snow from outside town through the street. It crawled and twisted down the street like snakes twenty feet high.

Ah Sam waited with his juggling gear in his hands.

"That's your cue," Ma whispered to me.

Here I was sleeping on the job again. Embarrassed, I put the harmonica to my mouth and began to play.

Ah Sam started to juggle the cups and balls. They circled over his head, always landing in his hands. As they went up and down, they formed pretty patterns in the air.

However, when Ah Sam tried to add the knives into the air, they stayed in his hands. The balls bounced on the ground, and the cups cracked.

Ah Sam lowered the knives. "I'm sorry. The metal handles are stuck to my palms."

Mr. Schultz shot to his feet. He spoke with a thick accent because he had just come to America, but he could talk loud. "Let him get closer to the fire," he said.

The whole crowd shuffled around so the bonfire was between them and Ah Sam.

I'd retreated farther back. As Ah Sam warmed himself by the fire, I reckoned I'd entertain the audience with more music. In his honor, I figured I'd play his favorite tune, "Sweet and Low."

However, the moment the harmonica touched my lips, the cold metal stuck. It was freezing this far away from the bonfire. I tried to dart for the station. Too late.

Mr. Schultz came over with a big grin. "We got to have music too."

My harmonica was stuck to my lips, and I kept my hands on it. Between it and my mittens, my face was still covered.

I tried to tell Mr. Schultz to go away, but the harmonica got in the way of talking. All I could do was mumble into the harmonica.

"Wait," Ma said to Mr. Schultz as he wrapped his bearlike arms around me.

However, he had already hoisted me into the air. "Here comes the band," he announced as he carried me over in front of the crowd by the fire.

I wanted to run into the house, but Ah Sam whispered, "Ursula, we need you."

I tried to curl up into a little ball as I muttered from around my harmonica, "I can't."

Ah Sam turned to the audience. "Don't we need our band?" he asked them.

They clapped real loud. At first I didn't know what for. My eyes darted around.

"Huzzah!" shouted Susie, and gave me the secret pirate sign for welcome.

It took awhile for it to sink in: All the applause and smiling faces were for me. And they kept it up until I felt my harmonica get loose between my lips.

In all the ruckus, I hadn't noticed my scarf was untied; but then it slid right off my shoulders. I didn't bother to pick it up, though.

To my crew I gave the secret pirate sign for "No

quarter." Pirate Ursula was back. And whether she was ramming Deadly Dan the Viceroy or playing the harmonica, Pirate Ursula did everything at full speed and without mercy.

"I'm ready anytime you are, Ursula," Ah Sam said. He had gathered up his balls.

I began to play sea chanteys, since Pirate Ursula had returned. At the same time, Ah Sam started to juggle the balls. When he added the knives, they flashed in the sunlight.

I wish that bald donkey man could have seen Ah Sam. He wouldn't have called my friend a coward now. Ah Sam was fearless as he snatched knives from the air and tossed them back up again.

"Does anyone in the audience have anything they want to add to my collection?" Ah Sam invited.

Tom threw in his big hat, and it began to dance with everything else. A huge turnip joined it. I wondered who had been carrying that thing around.

Mr. Schultz jerked off a boot, and soon that was bobbing merrily up and down too.

"Who'd have thought my boot was so talented?" Mr. Schultz hooted in delight as he wrapped his scarf around his stockinged foot.

And I saw that Ah Sam was right. It didn't matter how big or small a circus was. The magic came from inside. And it could touch even ordinary things like boots

and turnips and hats and make them dance in the air like they were alive.

When Ah Sam signaled me to stop, he told the audience, "What is a circus without at least one animal? So now, especially for Ursula, we have a Chinese lion."

And from our station Lung rolled out a ball big as him. Prancing behind him was the Chinese lion. It looked more like a big shaggy dog with long fur, but it had lots of teeth.

When Lung had stepped out of the way, the lion hopped on top of the ball. Then it rolled all around and did tricks. It even scratched itself and tried to bite fleas like a real lion. In the meantime Lung and Ah Sam had been setting up rows of poles. For its finale the lion leaped from one tall pole to another. When the lion hopped down from the ball, Ah Loo and Ah Bing got out of the costume.

They were sure talented folk. I never would have guessed it was two people doing the jumps together.

"And now for our final trick," Ah Sam said. "It is something all new. No one has ever seen it before," he proclaimed, and his cousins started to twist themselves into all kinds of shapes. They didn't seem to have a bone in their bodies.

Ah Sam whispered to me, "This is their new trick." And they began to turn into letters. Ah Bing became a "T" and Ah Loo became an "H" and somehow Lung became an "A."

Slowly they spelled out, "Thank You, Ursula."

The applause sounded like a dozen thunderstorms now. I felt my face burning a bright red.

Ah Sam nudged me. "In China performers thank the audience, too," he said. So he and I and his cousins faced the audience and began to clap.

"Did you plan this all the time?" I whispered back.

"It just happened," Ah Sam insisted innocently. "Blame it on the magic—circus magic."

And I left it at that. Because sometimes the magic changes you on the outside and turns a cook into a juggler.

And sometimes it changes you on the inside and turns a monster back into a person.

CHAPTER 10

Snow

That night I went to sleep dog tired but happy. Pirate Ursula was raring to sail again. Tomorrow I'd round up Cutthroat Peter and Killer Susie and the rest of my crew for new voyages around the Back of Beyond. I had a lot of adventures to catch up on.

When I woke up Sunday morning, it was still almost dark. I lifted the curtain. I decided to ask Ma to put back the old curtains. Outside, the snow was falling in long strings of ivory beads. It was already piled up high in the street.

I got out of bed and nearly jumped back under the quilt again. The floor was like ice. I hurried into my clothes and then went into the dining room.

Now that the show was over, Ah Sam's cousins had taken down the rope and blankets. The lion, the benches—

the whole circus—were packed up again in the boxes and trunks. It made me a little sad to realize the magic would be leaving with them.

I touched a big box, wondering if the lion was sleeping inside.

Ma came out of the kitchen. "I thought I heard you." Then she came over. "Everyone's in there where it's warm."

Pa was sipping some hot chocolate by the stove. "There won't be any stagecoach today in this snow. So you might as well take it easy today."

Ah Sam stirred a big pot of porridge. "Will it leave tomorrow?" he asked, worried.

Pa shook his head. "I doubt it. This is a regular blizzard. It could last for days."

That bothered Ah Sam. "Then we'll miss New Year's."

"Can't you hold the party later?" I asked.

"For us, New Year's is your Christmas and a lot of other holidays rolled into one," Ah Sam explained.

"Really?" I asked. "What do you do for New Year's?"

Ah Sam sighed. "Lots of things. Some important for Heaven. But we do other things, like eat lots, clean our houses. Men get haircuts. Maybe they trim their queue a little. And they shave the crowns off their heads. Anyone who has debts pays up. And we put money in red envelopes and give them out to children. We set off fireworks and beat gongs to scare away the bad spirits and have a dragon parade."

I felt bad at that.

"I'm right sorry," I said.

When Ah Sam finished speaking to his cousins, they looked even sadder than him. Lung began to rub his eyes something fierce and scrunch up his nose like he was fetching to cry.

That just about broke my heart after all they had done for us. If it hadn't been for me, they would have been able to enjoy New Year's with their friends. And that made me feel almost as miserable as Lung.

But then the more I thought about it, the more I realized Chinese New Year's was just the sort of holiday for Pirate Ursula and her crew. There were whole lots of eating and hollering and thunder and loot.

I reckoned what adventure Pirate Ursula and her crew would play next. Chinese New Year's would be our best game of all.

I tried to sound real casual, but inside I was boiling with excitement. "So what's this dragon parade like?"

Ah Sam talked while I wolfed down my breakfast porridge and toast. Then I excused myself and put on my coat and boots. I wound my scarf around my head to keep out the cold.

When I first opened the door, I nearly gave up. The snow came to my waist. Then I remembered Ah Sam trying to juggle knives that had frozen to his hands. If a little cold didn't stop him, I wasn't going to let a little snow make me hide. Pirate Ursula had hunkered inside long enough.

I could see when I set out; but a wind commenced to blow in true Back of Beyond fashion. And it was like the sky dropped buckets of snow. All the buildings grew blurry. I floundered along for a few more yards and then headed for the nearest place. I kept one hand on the wooden wall to guide me. "No quarter," I kept muttering to myself.

Cutthroat Peter was eating a dried apple in his living room. His pa was smoking a pipe in front of the chimney and reading.

They both jumped when I tapped at the window. Mr. Schultz opened the front door right away. "Come in, child. Come in. What would bring anyone out on a day like this?"

I stamped the snow off my boots first and stepped inside. I was grateful to be in the warmth and the light.

When I pulled down my scarf, Cutthroat Peter grinned. "Ursula."

"I'm spreading the word to the crew, Peter," I said, and gave him the secret sign for a new adventure.

"Pirate Ursula is back?" Peter asked excitedly. "Now things are really going to hop."

Mr. Schultz's laugh boomed through the room. "Ursula, if I'd known you were a pirate, I wouldn't have let you in."

"We're going to celebrate Chinese New Year's when the snow's done," I explained to him. "So the first thing Peter needs is to cut his hair. That's part of it."

"But we're not Chinese," Peter pointed out.

The steam was already beginning to rise from my clothing in the warm room. "But Ah Sam and his cousins are. They wanted to celebrate it in the Chinatown in the city, but the blizzard caught them."

"Those nice circus people?" asked Mr. Schultz.

"And they're real sad," I said. "So I thought we'd try to cheer them up. The blizzard is the perfect time to start getting ready."

"Will you cut my hair, Papa?" Peter asked Mr. Schultz. He was the town barber.

"Of course," Mr. Schultz puffed at his pipe. "In fact, I'll cut anyone's hair for free."

"That's right kind," I said. "Now I got to make my rounds."

Mr. Schultz replied, "In this weather? Why don't you stay with us?"

"Adventures don't wait," I said. "You got to hop on when they come round."

Mr. Schultz stretched. "I feel like taking my constitutional. Mind if I walk with you?"

"Aren't you too busy?" I asked. Mr. Schultz was an adult, after all. And adults never had a moment for games.

"For those nice folks I'll make time," Mr. Schultz promised. "They put on quite a show." He stomped his

boot. "I didn't know this old thing had so much talent till I saw it flying around in the air. I'm going to give all my clothes a lot more respect. My kitchen equipment too." Mr. Schultz winked at me.

I wasn't sure what to make of that, but I assumed he was just trying to pay a compliment to Ah Sam and his cousins.

Mr. Schultz got dressed while Peter and I drew up lists for each of the crew.

"You've got your orders, Cutthroat Peter," I said, pointing to his set.

"Aye, aye, Captain," Peter said, looking at his list.

When Mr. Schultz and I stepped outside, he tilted back his head and stuck out his tongue.

"Ah, fresh snow," he laughed. Right then Mr. Schultz didn't seem like Peter's father. He seemed more like an older brother.

I copied him and felt the snowflakes melting on my tongue. Suddenly I felt myself hoisted into the air.

"I'll carry you," Mr. Schultz said.

"But I can walk," I protested.

"A scrawny little thing like you? These winter breezes will carry you off to the Sandwich Isles. You come to our house for dinner. We'll put some meat on your bones," Mr. Schultz promised.

I felt like I was floating on a big, sturdy merchant ship as he plowed through the snow straight to Killer Susie's. When we got there, I made the sign for a new adventure.

Killer Susie gave a little excited jump and signed back.

However, before we could go off to talk, Mr. Schultz called in her whole family. "Ursula's got something to say to all of you."

I felt a little shy. "I only need to speak to Susie."

The snowflakes on Mr. Schultz's beard were melting. They left little wet stripes on his coat. "No, no, they'll all want to listen. Tell them about Chinese New Year's."

"Yes, we'd like to hear, dear," Susie's mother said.

I explained about Ah Sam and his cousins. I finished by saying, "So I thought we'd hold a little celebration for them."

"Ursula has a list of things to do," said Mr. Schultz.

"This is a long list," Susie's mother said when she read it.

Susie's father studied the list over her shoulder. "Making the dragon will be the hardest, though."

I reckoned they were right. Chinese New Year's wasn't your easy sort of holiday. Pirate Ursula and her crew were going to need help. And according to the books, when pirates needed somebody, they went to the nearest street and grabbed them.

"But Susie's always bragging about how good you sew, ma'am." I winked at my friend.

She piped right up. "Everyone knows it."

Her mother bit her lip. "Well, if it's for those nice folks, I guess I could help. What does the dragon look like?"

I tried to describe what Ah Sam had told me.

Susie's mother looked thoughtful. "Well, I have some old sheets. If we got some more from other folks, we could sew them together. Then we'd have enough for a good long dragon."

"Wonderful," Mr. Schultz boomed, and turned to me. "What color is the dragon, Ursula?"

"Red, I think. "

"We could dye it," said Susie's mother.

"Tom knows about all sorts of plants for dyes," Susie's father said.

"You mean you're going to help?" I asked, surprised.

"No one's going to call us ingrates," said Susie's mother.

"After all, they put on the circus for all of us," her father added.

Mr. Schultz winked. "Besides, it sounds like fun."

He wound up carrying me all around the town to the rest of the crew. At each place, though, I also drafted the adults.

"Is that everyone in the crew?" asked Mr. Schultz.

"Except for Klaus and Matilda," I said. Their farm was outside of town. "And there's John on the Circle-T. And Harry up at the mine."

"Tell me what you want them to do, Pirate Ursula," said Mr. Schultz, "and I'll tell Bill Anderson. He can hitch up a team to a sled and get out there." Mr. Anderson owned the livery stable.

"But he's not part of the crew," I said, puzzled. "He doesn't have any children."

"Yesterday Bill told me that he'd never had more fun in his life," Mr. Schultz said confidently. "When I tell him what you told me, he'll go." He tapped his chin. "There's a few other folks he should tell too."

"I don't want anyone to go to any trouble," I said, worried.

"It's no trouble, Ursula," Mr. Schultz said, and made a neighing sound. "Now your ancient steed will carry you home." As he began to plod through the snow, he laughed loudly over the wind. "Peter's right. When Pirate Ursula's around, things really hop."

CHAPTER 11

The Magic

When I got home, everyone except Lung was dressed in coats and boots. Ma grabbed me as soon as I walked in through the door. Then she started to scold me. "Ursula, where have you been? We were all so worried."

Pa came over. "We were about to go out and look for you."

"I just wanted to round up folks. I thought we ought to hold Chinese New Year's for Ah Sam and his cousins," I explained.

"For us?" Ah Sam asked in amazement.

"What do *you* want to do, Ma?" I asked as I shed my coat and boots. "We still need sheets and folks to sew them together for the dragon."

"Well, I reckon I can't do much else with the blizzard

outside," Ma said, and tapped her fingers thoughtfully. "I'll dig some old sheets out of the closet."

I poked Pa in the ribs. "What about you?"

Pa scratched his head. "I was never much good with a needle, Sugar, but I'll try."

I wasn't going to give him a chance to weasel out, though. "A dragon's got to have a head too," I said, and turned to Ah Sam. "Say, how do we make that, anyway?"

Ah Sam plopped down in a chair as if this were all happening too fast. "You want to celebrate Chinese New Year's?"

"Well, it's our fault you're missing the one in China-town." I grinned.

Ah Sam twisted around and explained things to his cousins. Ah Bing and Ah Loo seemed just as surprised as Ah Sam. Lung even started to tear up all over again. He was a regular human water pump.

Those were busy times for Pirate Ursula. I had to make sure no one was shirking their duties. As I went around, though, I saw everyone was beginning to see it was a real lark.

Folks from all over brought in old white sheets or pieces of canvas to our station. Mr. Schultz even donated a couple of his nightshirts. "After all, they're big enough for ship sails," he said, chuckling.

Miss Hardy came in with sheets of her own and said her students could study fractions when the weather got better. In the meantime we could study China this way.

And then she sat down with Ma, Pa and the other parents of the crew. They sewed the sheets together in our dining room. Instead of a quilting bee, they called it a dragon bee. Eventually the body stretched along one wall, bent around and followed the next.

At the same time, Ah Sam and his cousins began to work on the dragon's head over in one corner. They were making the frame out of thin strips of wood. They used strips of rice paper and rice paste to glue them together.

In honor of Chinese New Year's Mr. Schultz had started to give free haircuts to the town. However, he'd gotten lonely in his shop, so he'd moved into our dining room, where he used a corner for his barbering.

When the wind was blowing the hardest, we heard a knocking at the door. When I opened it, I saw it was Tom with snowshoes on his feet.

"Come in," I said, taking his arm. "You must be freezing."

"I-I-I'm past that," he said through chattering teeth. Kicking off his snowshoes, he staggered into our station.

Mr. Schultz put down his scissors. "I didn't expect you to come until after the blizzard."

Tom took in the long, white dragon body. "I come to see the dragon. But it sure looks awfully pale."

"We've got to dye it somehow," I said.

Tom grinned. "Bill Anderson told me you might need some help with that. I thought you might need these to color it." He set down a bag full of pungent roots. "In this cold, it will take awhile to dry."

"The last thing we want is a wet dragon," Ah Sam agreed.

After we got some hot soup into Tom, he took over a cauldron and began to brew the dye. The smell would have made a skunk jealous. Tom was the only one who could stand to be in the kitchen while he did that. Then he fixed the dye with annis root so the red would stick to the cloth. If he didn't, it would come off on any sweaty hand.

It took Pa and a bunch of others to carry the dragon's body over to Mr. Anderson's stable. They drew straws about who was to carry the cauldron of dye there. Mr. Schultz was among the losers.

As they dyed yard after yard of the cloth, it came out a deep red. So did their hands. Tom said the dye would wear off—eventually.

When they hung the dragon up from the rafters, it looked like a huge scarlet cloud was trapped under the roof. Red rain pattered down steadily upon the dirt floor.

Back in the station we piled up the tables and station benches against one wall and put the circus's crates and trunks on top of them. When the floor had been cleared, Ah Sam and Ah Bing began to rehearse the dragon dancers. In China it would have been just the men, but Ma and some of the other mothers wanted to get in on the fun too.

"Well, this is a Whistle dragon," Ah Sam shrugged. "Why not?"

Lung brought out a big pot and beat the rhythm as they began to learn how to dance. They had to move and wind back and forth together. They took turns squatting so the dragon's body would look like it was curling up and down.

There was a lot of laughing while they practiced. And a lot of feet got stepped on accidentally too.

Ah Bing got real excited as he coached them. He seemed to forget most of his English. So the only two words he wound up using were "More high, more high!" Somehow Ah Sam always understood what his cousin meant. He always gave more detailed instructions.

While the dancers practiced, my crew and I cut up newspapers and made papier-mâché to cover the frame of the dragon's head. But we got as much flour and water on us as we did on the papier-mâché. Killer Susie looked like she was covered in whitewash.

In his corner of the station, hair of every color covered the floor up to Mr. Schultz's ankles.

Lung had put dents into the bottom of the pot as he banged out the rhythm.

In the meantime Pa had tripped over his own feet. About a dozen people had stumbled over him, including Ma.

She got to her feet and gave him a big kiss. "You've got a lot of virtues, but dancing was never one of them."

I stepped back for a moment and studied the head. "The dragon needs a face."

"Make it look like me," Peter said, and scowled ferociously.

Susie rubbed her chin. "Well, Peter Schultz, I wouldn't want to meet you on a dark night. But I don't know if you're up to being a dragon."

"Well, you try it," Peter shot back.

"Let's each take a turn and then vote," I suggested.

We each made faces, but then Mr. Schultz came over with his scissors still in his hand. "Me next, me next!"

He stretched his mouth wide enough to swallow us whole. And he boggled his eyes like a monster. I was so startled that I jumped back. Even Peter gulped.

It took me a moment to find my voice. "He could be the *King* of the Dragons."

Susie was so startled by the change that she stammered, "I-I vote for Mr. Schultz."

It was unanimous.

"Hey, what about my haircut?" the man called from his chair.

"In a moment," Mr. Schultz said. He raised his scissors like a sword and struck a pose. "The King of the Dragons cuts hair only when *he* wants to."

CHAPTER 12

New Year's

The snow was falling something fierce, so there weren't going to be any stagecoaches for a while yet. Even so, it was time to set our home right.

"As soon as we clean up, it's the station's turn," said Ma. "We have to prepare for New Year's."

When Ma gets into a rhythm, she can get rid of dirt faster than a dozen of these newfangled carpet sweepers. However, folks kept dropping by to settle little debts. At first Ma would apologize. "I'm such a fright," she'd say, pointing to the rag wrapped around her hair and her old dress.

Everyone else, though, was dressed just as shabbily because they had been cleaning their houses too. So after a while Ma stopped making excuses for her clothes.

Despite the howling wind and snow, Pa and Mr.

Anderson went out on his sled and were gone all day. They wanted to tell folks whom Mr. Anderson had missed on the earlier go-round.

In the meantime Ah Sam started to cook up a storm. So did everyone else. Whenever the wind blew against the station, I could smell all the cooking fires. Everyone was taking him seriously about having plenty of food to eat.

If it hadn't been so blustery outside, I could have skipped meals for a whole week. I could have gotten my fill by walking around town and inhaling the air.

That night as I snuggled underneath my quilt, I suddenly noticed something strange. It was quiet outside. I peeked through my old curtains. The sky had cleared enough for the moon to shine down. Outside, the snow had finally stopped.

At first I was afraid that Ah Sam and his cousins would light out right away for Chinatown. The snow, though, lay thick on the ground. It would take awhile for it to melt enough for the roads to reopen.

Wednesday morning folks from all around the county came to town. It was a bright, clear day, but cold. John and the cowboys from his family's ranch were bundled up as they rode in through the snow. Harry and the miners skied in with small barrels strapped to their backs.

Excited, I got dressed and skipped outside to the dining room. The dragon's head sat in one corner. It looked a lot like Mr. Schultz if he had had scales and fangs.

Inside the kitchen Ah Sam was sitting with his cousins. He looked tired but happy.

"We've been waiting for you," he said.

"Happy New Year," I said.

"Now for the most important lesson," said Ah Sam. "In Chinese you say *Goong hay fat choy*."

Lung helped me practice it a dozen times. Then I tried it on Ah Sam.

"Thank you," he said. From his pocket he took a small red rectangle and handed it to me. Inside I felt a coin. "I didn't have red envelopes, so I wrapped it in red paper."

"*Goong hay fat choy*," Lung said to him, and also got a rectangle.

"Now you wish it to my cousins," Ah Sam said, so I gave them the same greeting and got more rectangles with money. A pirate could get spoiled by this.

When my parents came in, Pa winked. "Don't you want to wish me something?"

I did it in both Chinese and English and got some more rectangles. So did Lung.

Cutthroat Peter and his mother came over a little while after that. "We thought we'd start here," he said.

"Where's your father?" I asked.

"Giving more free haircuts," Peter explained. "There are all those miners and cowboys who just came in."

I got some rectangles of money from his mother, and

Peter got rectangles of money from mine. Then Ah Sam got up. "I'd better finish cooking."

Ma, though, pushed him back toward the table. "Today's your holiday. I'll do the rest and serve you."

"But that's my job," protested Ah Sam.

"Not today," Ma said. "You just leave it to the cook of the fluffiest pancakes in the West."

By now everyone knew Ah Sam was the best cook, but we also knew enough to keep our mouths shut.

Once we had put on our coats, we commenced moving from building to building. Every place was spanking clean. And whether it was a store or a house, the owner insisted on serving Ah Sam and his cousins.

We ate our way across the town. Only poor Mr. Schultz didn't get to eat much, because he was still giving free haircuts. And at every building there was money wrapped in red paper for all the children.

Finally Mr. Schultz shut up shop late in the afternoon. "Enough's enough. A man's got to keep his figure." Fortunately there were still plenty of leftovers for him. Even so, he kept his scissors in his pocket. When someone came out to ask for a haircut, he would snip off a bit of his hair. "That's a good start for the New Year's. Come and see me tomorrow for the rest," he would say.

Finally Ah Sam started to call, "May I have all the dancers?"

When the group of twenty had gathered, they went

to the stable and then carried the long cloth back to the station. "It's still wet," Pa said, showing me his red palms.

"It can't be helped. It couldn't dry enough in this cold weather," said Ah Sam. He and Ah Bing attached the body to the head. But the cloth, lying on the floor, looked like a twisting river of blood. Right now the dragon looked more dead than alive.

Then Harry's father called everyone outside. "I'm told you need fireworks for Chinese New Year's. So this is our share for the show."

The miners broke open the kegs of gunpowder. They used it to make something they called cannon crackers. But they looked just like gigantic firecrackers to me.

Of course, I volunteered myself and the crew to set them off. However, Pa corralled me. "No, you don't. We can't stop you when you're full grown. But until then we're going to keep all your working parts together."

I watched enviously as the miners set off the explosions, sending up sprays of snow. My eyes were dazzled by the starbursts and my ears went numb from the thunder. Faintly I heard the tinkling of glass.

Pa was shouting, but his voice sounded only like a dim whisper. "They broke the windows on the hotel."

I looked where he was pointing. Six windows on the lower floor had shattered. I guess they'd packed some of the gunpowder a little too much.

While the miners boarded up the windows against

the cold, Ah Sam tried to gather the dancers again. At first he tried calling to them, but some of them had been deafened by the noise. So he wound up grabbing their arms and pointing to the station.

By the time he had everybody inside, my ears had started to clear. Ah Loo and Lung came out of the kitchen with every pot and lid they could carry.

"Ursula, can you hear me?" Ah Sam asked.

I slapped the side of my head. "There's still a little ringing, but I'm okay."

"I need you and your friends for the most important part," he explained.

"We're ready," I said, excited.

"We need your crew to be the drums and gongs," he said. "You'll set the beat for our feet."

Lung started to show us the rhythm. When Ah Sam was satisfied, he clapped his hands. "Dancers, take up your positions." Ah Loo stood by the head while Ah Bing got behind her. Ah Sam took his spot as the tail. Ma and Pa and the other dancers took up spots in between the two.

Then everyone squatted down. Ah Loo got under the head while the others scooted under the cloth. Suddenly the body started to fill out. When everyone stood up, it looked like the dragon had as many legs as a centipede.

Lung began to drum on the bottom of a pot. The rest of the crew banged lids together like cymbals or beat on other pots.

Dancing backward, Lung skipped through the door. And we marched behind him. The dragon danced out of our station after us.

The crowd outside started to applaud. The dragon pranced about the street. Ah Loo had the head, and sometimes she'd stand on her husband's shoulders. Then it looked like the front part of the dragon was rearing up. Some of it was more like the lion dance, but no one complained.

Mrs. Turnbull, who had gone to bed early, got quite a scare when she found a dragon grinning at her through her second-story window.

There was never a dragon like it.

There was never a New Year's like it.

Ah Sam was right. The magic came from inside, not outside. And it had been like throwing a penny into a pond. The ripples had just spread and spread until they had touched everyone.

We hit a warming spell the next day. The snow began melting all over real quick, and in a couple of days a stagecoach came rolling in. Everyone was right sorry when Ah Sam's cousins left. Before they got on the stagecoach, they went to each building in town and bowed and said something in Chinese.

After that I started to go to school again, and no one made fun of me. Instead, they asked me to play the circus music again. And I did.

I learned lots more tunes, too. Folks around town were only too happy to teach me. I have to get ready for the circus next year. Ah Sam says it will be even bigger and better.

But they still need me.

AFTERWORD

Chinese American history in the last half of the nine-teenth century and the early twentieth century makes for pretty grim reading. So when I read Elliot Paul's memoir, *A Ghost Town on the Yellowstone*, this sweet, cheerful story leaped out at me.

Since this is fiction, I've taken a few liberties for dramatic purposes. Though there was no Ursula, there was an epidemic that disfigured a number of people, including an attractive young woman. And there were two Chinese cooks, not one.

Otherwise, though, I have followed the real events that occurred in Trembles, Montana, including the Native American who helped make the dragon.

I wish to thank Steven Doi, who sent me a copy of *A Ghost Town on the Yellowstone*.

SWEET AND LOW.

CRADLE SONG.

Words by TENNYSON

Music by MRS. R. H. ALEXANDER.

Andante tranquillo.

PIANO.

Sweet and low, Sweet and low Wind of the west — ern sea.
Sleep and rest, Sleep and rest Father will come to thee soon.

Low, low, breathe and blow Wind of the west — ern sea.
Rest, rest, on mother's breast Father will come to thee soon.

Sweet and low sweet and low Wind of the west — ern sea
Sleep and rest sleep and rest Father will come to thee soon

Low low breathe and blow Wind of the west — ern sea....
Rest rest on mother's breast Father will come to thee soon....